'Dr Craven, you're needed in Resus One,' the nurse said. 'Patient just admitted…young child…rescued from a house fire…extensive burns to his legs. Jack Harvey is in charge.'

Anna put on a spurt and headed briskly into the resus room.

Jack looked up and experienced a chilling shock at the woman who so resembled Claire walked into the room.

'Glad of your assistance, Dr Craven,' he said, keeping his voice on an even keel even though his heart had gone into overdrive. He'd get used to it, he told himself, working with her on a daily basis—and the shock waves would become less each time they met. Or maybe not…because these particular shock waves were becoming very pleasurable, he had to admit.

'We're prepping this young patient for a transfusion,' he told her. 'The burns are so bad that he needs blood as soon as possible or there's a good chance he'll die of shock.'

At that moment the monitors surrounding the boy began to bleep erratically. 'Get the defibrillator here,' Jack shouted. 'He's arrested!'

Barbara Hart was born in Lancashire and educated at a convent in Wales. At twenty-one she moved to New York, where she worked as an advertising copy writer. After two years in the USA she returned to England to become a television press officer in charge of publicising a top soap opera and a leading current affairs programme. She gave up her job to write novels. She lives in Cheshire and is married to a solicitor. They have two grown-up sons.

Recent titles by the same author:

THE DOCTOR'S LOVE-CHILD
ENGAGING DR DRISCOLL

THE EMERGENCY SPECIALIST

BY

BARBARA HART

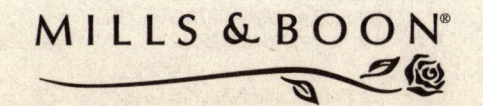

MILLS & BOON

To my sister, Phyllis

DID YOU PURCHASE THIS BOOK WITHOUT A COVER?
If you did, you should be aware it is **stolen property** as it was reported *unsold and destroyed* by a retailer. Neither the author nor the publisher has received any payment for this book.

All the characters in this book have no existence outside the imagination of the author, and have no relation whatsoever to anyone bearing the same name or names. They are not even distantly inspired by any individual known or unknown to the author, and all the incidents are pure invention.

All Rights Reserved including the right of reproduction in whole or in part in any form. This edition is published by arrangement with Harlequin Enterprises II B.V. The text of this publication or any part thereof may not be reproduced or transmitted in any form or by any means, electronic or mechanical, including photocopying, recording, storage in an information retrieval system, or otherwise, without the written permission of the publisher.

This book is sold subject to the condition that it shall not, by way of trade or otherwise, be lent, resold, hired out or otherwise circulated without the prior consent of the publisher in any form of binding or cover other than that in which it is published and without a similar condition including this condition being imposed on the subsequent purchaser.

MILLS & BOON and MILLS & BOON with the Rose Device are registered trademarks of the publisher.

First published in Great Britain 2002
Harlequin Mills & Boon Limited,
Eton House, 18-24 Paradise Road, Richmond, Surrey TW9 1SR

© Barbara Hart 2002

ISBN 0 263 83423 9

Set in Times Roman 10½ on 12 pt.
03-0103-45612

Printed and bound in Spain
by Litografia Rosés, S.A., Barcelona

CHAPTER ONE

IT HAD been a hard morning's work at the Royal's accident and emergency department. During a lull in dealing with patients, duty registrar Anna Craven told her colleagues that she was taking a short lunch-break.

'If I don't get something to eat in the next three minutes I'll pass out on the floor,' she said, walking in the direction of the staff canteen.

She grabbed a sandwich and a can of lemonade and went to sit by herself at a table in the far corner, away from the main seating area which always seemed to be crowded and noisy. She liked to spend the rare moments away from A and E in as tranquil an area as possible. Often, if the canteen was busier than usual, she'd take her sandwiches out to her car and sit there in solitude, the car radio tuned in to a classical station.

Friends and colleagues often remarked on how serene Anna always looked. With her smooth blonde hair, her pale green eyes and her delicate bone structure, she appeared to all the world to be the very embodiment of calmness. How deceptive appearances could be! The outer calm took a lot of working on and quite frequently hid inner turmoil underneath.

Anna had two sisters and both of them were just the opposite of her. They even looked different. Instead of straight blonde hair, Rebecca and Jennifer had naturally curly raven locks. And whereas Anna was diplomatic, her sisters were extremely outspoken to the point of rudeness, saying exactly what they thought without a care in the world that they might hurt anybody's feelings.

'I suppose you're the way you are because you're the middle child,' Rebecca had said. 'I'm the eldest and the bossy one. Jenny, being the youngest, is the spoiled brat...and you're the poor child caught in the middle. Either that or you were potty-trained too early!'

Rebecca and Jennifer were both married...happily married, Anna presumed, although sometimes she did wonder, the way they constantly grumbled about their spouses and their children, each sister trying to outdo the other with awful stories. One thing was for sure— they were desperately keen that Anna should get married and then she'd be 'just like us'. It seemed to annoy them immensely that while they were stuck at home with young families, their footloose and fancy-free sister was, they imagined, living the life of Riley as a single 'career girl'.

'I bet you'd soon lose your composure if you'd got three kids under four playing merry hell all day,' suggested Rebecca, unable to comprehend how anyone could stay as calm and unflappable as Anna.

Anna's outward composure confused others, particularly men. Deep inside her, she knew she was a passionate, fervent human being, capable of deep, heartfelt emotions. She also had a lively mind and a good sense of humour, appreciating wit more than slapstick. But she found it difficult, embarrassing even, to make a public display of her feelings.

Even now, when she was feeling utterly wretched because of Liam, she couldn't bring herself to confide in anyone. Telling her colleagues was just asking to get talked about by the gossip-mongers, and sharing her misery with her sisters would only have served to increase the pain instead of halving it. No, the loss of Liam was something she'd have to cope with on her own, hiding it under a guise of tight-lipped tranquillity. Liam, who had taken her love and tossed it aside without even realising what he'd done. Liam, whom she'd fallen in love with and whom she'd thought had fallen in love with her. But that was the problem with being cool and serene on the outside...it often sent out the wrong message. It made people believe that you were hard and indifferent to personal pain.

'No commitments,' he'd said from time to time during their six months together, his eyes smiling at her, always smiling. 'We're having a great time, aren't we?' And he'd laughed charmingly. He was the most charming man she'd ever met. She realised with hindsight that his charm meant nothing. It was unintentional and came as naturally to him as breathing. Easy come, easy go. He had probably no idea, not even now, that he'd hurt her almost more than she'd been able to bear.

'You mustn't take me seriously,' he'd warned her. But she had. She'd taken him very seriously. And when, only two weeks ago, Rebecca had said once again, 'You really should get married, Anna,' she'd *almost* told her that she was seeing Liam and that maybe marriage was on the cards.

She was so glad that she hadn't told either of her sisters about Liam. Knowing Rebecca and Jennifer, they would have booked the church and the reception and arranged between themselves which of their various children should be bridesmaids and pageboys!

She thanked her stars she hadn't mentioned him to them because only a few days later Liam had confessed to her that he was seeing someone else. The news had come as a tremendous shock.

'But we weren't serious, were we? We had a good laugh, didn't we?' he'd said. At least he'd had the decency to look embarrassed at his bad behaviour. 'We can still be friends, can't we?'

It had been at that point she'd been grateful for her cool exterior. With her heart pounding like mad, her stomach churning so much that she'd felt sick, she'd still been able to give him a half-smile as she'd said, 'No, Liam. I'm afraid we can't.'

Anna finished her lunch and left the canteen. With her mind still on Liam and the pain he had so carelessly inflicted on her, she made her way back to A and E. She was preoccupied with thoughts of her broken romance when she became aware of the sound of quickening footsteps behind her. She stepped to one side, thinking that somebody might want to get past in a hurry. Then a man said, 'Anneka?' Looking round, she saw that the man, a medic she presumed from his theatre blues, was talking to her.

'Are you speaking to me?' she asked.

She found herself looking into the brown eyes of a man she'd never seen before, though that was hardly surprising in a hospital the size of the Royal. He was tall and dark-haired, and good-looking. Even under his theatre garb she could see that his shoulders were wide and powerful, his body lean and tapering. His skin was slightly bronzed as if he'd just returned from a holiday abroad. But underneath the tan he looked pale...a very strange illusion, thought Anna. She'd seen it before in patients who were in shock. All the colour drained from their faces, but a little of the tan remained.

The man stood stock still, staring at her. He said nothing, just stared at her. She felt herself shiver under his gaze.

'Are you all right?' she asked. 'You look as if you've seen a ghost.'

'I'm sorry,' he said. 'You just reminded me of someone else.' He appeared embarrassed by his gaffe.

To smooth things over, she gave him a brief smile, saying, 'My name's Anna. I thought at first that you'd just got my name wrong. Is it someone called Anneka you're looking for?'

The man half turned away, not rudely. 'Sorry about that,' he said, walking back down the corridor. 'I'm supposed to be in Theatre. Sorry to have bothered you.'

Anna shrugged her shoulders and continued on her way.

The rest of the day was just as hectic as the morning had been.

A young boy who'd broken his arm in two places was X-rayed and his arm set in plaster. He was sent home with an 'I Was Brave' sticker on his shirt and a prescription for child analgesic. A pregnant woman with stomach pains and white with fear that she would lose her baby was examined, given tests and then admitted to a ward for observation. There were two drunks and a drug addict, a man with toothache and a middle-aged woman who'd injured herself during an epileptic fit. They were arriving in a steady trickle on foot, by car and by ambulance.

'We've got a stabbing coming in now,' said the sister in charge of the day team as she ran to the ambulance entrance.

A surgeon and an operating department assistant had been bleeped but they hadn't yet arrived. Two radiographers, three nurses and Anna were waiting in one of the resuscitation wards.

When the patient arrived, his clothes covered in blood, he was raving and abusive but otherwise co-operative.

'I'll kill the bastards who did this,' he shouted, his voice slurred with drink and pain. 'I thought they were going to hit me with a bottle but they stabbed me instead. In the bloody back! The cowardly bastards!'

'Roll him over,' instructed Anna in order that the team could examine the injury. Above their heads the incident clock logged the seconds.

After an initial examination, the radiographers X-rayed him and a nurse monitored his blood pressure.

'Here comes the surgery team,' said the sister in charge. Anna looked round briefly and saw that the surgeon walking towards them and their blood-soaked patient was the man who'd come running after her in the corridor earlier that day, calling her 'Anneka'.

'Hello again,' she said. 'I'm Anna Craven, the duty registrar.'

'Jack Harvey,' he replied in acknowledgement, 'the new casualty consultant.' He smiled at her and nodded to the rest of the team.

Anna told him the patient's history and said they

were now waiting for the X-rays to come back. They arrived almost as she spoke and Anna and Jack studied them.

'His chest cavity is filling with blood,' said Jack. 'His lungs will be getting squashed and he'll have difficulty in breathing if we don't drain it straight away.'

The team worked swiftly and efficiently, draining the patient's chest and stemming the blood flow from the stab wound. It took them less than thirty minutes to stabilise his condition and get him out of immediate danger.

During the time they worked together, Anna noticed that Jack kept looking at her—not in a blatantly sexual way—but more out of curiosity. She couldn't help noticing him either. He really was very good-looking. He reminded her in some ways of Liam—but whereas Liam had pale blue eyes, Jack's were a warm brown.

When the surgeon and his operating assistant had left, taking the wounded patient with them, one of the nurses said to Anna, 'He's a bit of a dish, isn't he?'

'You mean our stab victim? A bit too heavy-jowled for me,' said Anna, deliberately misunderstanding.

'Not him! I mean Mr Handsome, the new casualty consultant.'

'Handsome is as handsome does,' replied Anna, smiling through gritted teeth, adding, 'I'm right off good-looking men at the moment. In fact, I'm off all men, full stop.'

'Yeah, me too,' said the nurse. 'They're all pigs, aren't they?'

* * *

At the end of her shift, Anna changed out of the theatre blues worn by all the doctors and nurses in A and E and into her own clothes.

She was walking to her car when, for the second time that day, she heard someone running towards her. And again it was Jack Harvey.

'Anna!' he said, calling to her from several metres away.

A prickle of irritation went through her. She wasn't in the mood for talking, not to him or anyone. She just wanted to get home to the safe haven of her small apartment and continue the healing process on her own. The hurt inflicted by Liam was still very raw and it was going to take longer than a couple of weeks to heal. For that she needed to be by herself. Solitary confinement had a lot going for it, she decided. By the time Jack had reached her she'd taken out her car key and was fitting it in the lock, ready for a quick getaway.

'Anna,' he said again when he reached her. He was slightly breathless, having sprinted at top speed across the full length of the car park.

'At least you've got my name right this time!' she joked through clenched teeth.

He took a deep breath. 'Will you come out for a drink with me?' he asked, the words tumbling out all at once.

'What? Now?' She tried to keep the irritation from her voice.

He nodded.

The nerve of the man! The nerve of all handsome men! They just think they can snap their fingers and you'll come running.

'Sorry,' she said, 'got things to do.'

She opened the car door and slid into the driver's seat.

'Another night, then?' he persisted, leaning into the car. 'Perhaps we could have a meal?' He looked so intense, so appealing and little-boy-lost that Anna almost weakened.

'I'm afraid you'll have to take no for an answer, Jack,' she said pleasantly but firmly, her cool, serene looks emphasising that she really did mean no.

'Look,' he said, putting a gentle hand on her arm and fixing her with penetrating eyes, 'you don't understand. I'm in a bit of a state of shock right now. I've been in shock since I saw you coming out of the canteen earlier today. You see, you reminded me so much of someone else. That's why I looked as if I'd seen a ghost.'

He was persistent all right, thought Anna. But although she wasn't going to let him bamboozle her into a date, she was becoming a little curious about him.

'You called me Anneka,' she said. As she spoke the name she noticed that he flinched slightly as if she'd hit him. 'Is that who I look like? Is she an ex-girlfriend or something?'

He stood stock still for a moment. 'Anneka was my wife,' he said quietly. 'She died three years ago.'

Anna was now the one who felt as if she'd been struck.

'Oh, I'm sorry.' She kept her cool exterior but inside she was cringing because of the flippant way she'd been treating him, imagining that he was just trying to pick her up.

'I've seen blonde women who looked a little like her,' he said, 'but until today I've never met anyone who could have been her double. It gave me a very nasty turn. I thought I was starting to hallucinate.' He laughed a hollow laugh.

The haunting look of pain on his face won her over. 'I'm sorry, Jack,' she said. 'I really can't make it tonight, but I probably can tomorrow. Just for a quick drink.'

His face lost its tension and he smiled almost with relief.

'Thanks,' he said, before turning and walking away.

She drove home pensively. For the first time in two weeks her mind, outside working hours, was not on Liam and her broken heart. Jack's loss had put her own pain in perspective. When Liam had left her it had felt almost like a bereavement. But, of course, she knew it wasn't *really* like someone dying because that was so final, so sad. It had been three years, he'd said, since his wife's death and still Jack had the mark of pain and suffering imprinted on his face. If seeing someone who looked like your dead wife had the power to make you react in such an obsessive and compelling manner *after three years*, how long was it going to take the poor man to finally get over his loss?

In some perverse way she found Jack's situation faintly reassuring. Hopefully, she wasn't going to be pining after Liam in three years' time. Maybe solitary confinement wasn't the complete answer for her. Perhaps going out with Jack could be another way of helping her in her own healing process?

The following evening, after they'd both finished their day shifts, they went out for a drink. Anna had come into work on the bus that morning, knowing that she would be given a lift home. Jack, although he'd only recently joined the Royal as the new casualty surgeon, was not a stranger to the area and he knew several pubs within a few miles of the hospital. He drove to one of the quieter inns, playing a classical music tape as they drove along.

'That's nice,' she said conversationally. 'It's one of my favourites.'

He parked the car and turned off the engine.

'I know all the drinking dives round here from my days as a medical student,' he said as they got out of the car and walked towards the pub. 'This one didn't come high on our list. We used to head for the pubs with loud music, cheap beer and greasy food!'

Anna raised her eyebrows in alarm.

'Don't worry, this one's just the opposite. No piped music, real ale and decent food,' he reassured her.

'But this is only for a drink?' asked Anna, checking that he wasn't trying to make it more of a date than she'd intended. She'd only agreed to go out with him because he'd mentioned that he'd lost his wife. For the foreseeable future she wasn't planning on dating anyone...she was too bruised emotionally even to consider it.

'Just a quick drink,' he confirmed, adding with an amused grin, 'I'm not going to press-gang you into a romantic candlelit dinner.'

He chose a secluded corner for them and then went to the bar to get their drinks. A few minutes later he returned with two glasses.

'One white wine,' he said, putting the glass of chilled Chardonnay on the small, marble-topped table alongside his pint.

'Cheers!' they said in unison.

Jack watched her like a hawk, his eyes never leaving her even as he took a long swig of his beer. She found his scrutiny unnerving.

'So,' she said lightly, 'you're no stranger to this area?'

'No. But I don't remember too much about it, if I'm being frank. After all, I was a student and I was working very long hours. But the area does have happy memories for me. That's one reason I applied for this surgical post when I saw it advertised.'

This area used to have happy memories for me, too, brooded Anna, but at that moment she couldn't think of a single one. The break-up with Liam seemed to have obliterated every happy memory she'd ever had.

'So tell me about yourself,' he asked. 'Are you from round here?'

Anna had been dreading this from the moment she'd agreed to go out with him for a drink. She hated being cross-examined about her personal life at the best of times, and she hated it even more now—at the worst of times.

'Oh, you don't want to hear about me,' she said, giving him a smile that she hoped came across as genuine. 'Tell me more about yourself. I'm sure that's much more interesting. Tell me about those happy memories.'

He didn't answer immediately, fixing her with one of his penetrating looks. Then, slowly, he smiled, his face lighting up as his eyes seemed to caress her face, her hair, her shoulders.

'You really are so like her,' he murmured almost in a whisper. Then he shook his head as if to bring himself back to the present moment.

'I was a medical student here, as I've already told you. And even though it was extremely hard work and long hours, I still look back on those times as the happiest in my life. Mostly, I suppose, because that's when I met Anneka. She was working as an au pair to a local family.'

'How did you meet her?' Anna asked gently, aware of the shaft of pain that had crossed his face.

'She used to go out on her evenings off with two other Danish au pairs. They used to join in with the groups of students that congregated around the pubs and bars. I fell for her the moment I first saw her. I offered to buy her a drink and was stunned when all three of them said, "Yes, please," and proceeded to order the most expensive cocktails from the flashy barman. I couldn't afford to eat for the rest of that week! When I'd saved up a bit of cash I plucked up the courage to ask her out, making sure the other two were well out of earshot.'

'Did you sometimes bring her here?' asked Anna wondering if he'd deliberately chosen this particular pub to try and re-create his time with Anneka.

'No,' he replied. 'She used to like the loud disco music and noisy student atmosphere of the other pubs...the ones I avoided tonight.'

'She was a bit of a raver, was she?' Anna asked, beginning to draw a picture in her mind of a woman with her own blonde-haired looks but with a totally different personality.

'Weren't we all?' Jack laughed, casting his mind back to his mad student days. 'She liked partying into the night—and almost got fired from her job because of it!'

'Oh, dear,' said Anna, deciding that she and his

late wife would have had very little in common apart from the blonde hair.

Jack was still in the happy world of the past as he recalled the angry scene on the doorstep between Anneka and her employer when he'd taken her home in the early hours of the morning after a particularly riotous all-night party.

Anna and Jack had been in the pub less than an hour. Anna finished her wine and glanced at her watch.

'I ought to be getting home soon,' she said, hoping that he wouldn't cross-examine her on why she needed to be leaving so soon. She hadn't worked out a convincing answer and was relieved when he too said it was time he was on his way. It wasn't that she found his company boring, far from it. There was something magnetic about him and, if she hadn't been so traumatised by her recent break-up, she might have found herself falling for him.

They walked into the pub car park, saying very little, preoccupied with their own thoughts. When they were in the car he put the key in the ignition and started the engine. Then he switched it off. He turned towards her and put his arm round the back of her seat.

Oh, God, she thought, *he's going to kiss me.*

Before she could make up her mind about how she was going to handle the situation, it turned out he wasn't intent on kissing her at all—he was only trying to get at his mobile phone.

'Would you mind if I made a quick phone call?' he asked.

'No, please do,' she said, relief flooding over her. He was a gorgeous, handsome man, with a sexy voice, and no doubt most other women would have been delighted for him to kiss them, but not Anna. She was completely immune to his obvious charms...indeed, she was completely immune to any man's charms. She must have a heart in there somewhere, but she felt as if it was made of stone.

Jack retrieved his mobile from a bag he'd placed behind her seat. He dialled a number which was answered almost immediately.

'Hi, it's me,' he said. 'I'm on my way home. Is there anything you need me to pick up from the shops on the way back?'

He paused while the person at the other end replied.

'OK,' he said, 'just some yoghurts. Is strawberry still her favourite?'

Another pause.

'Fine. See you in a few minutes.' He ended the call and replaced the mobile in his bag.

Anna didn't show any curiosity about the phone call. Her mind was elsewhere, conjuring up images of Liam, wondering what he was doing right now.

Jack started the car again. 'I was just phoning my housekeeper,' he explained. 'Damn, I meant to ask her if Saskia was still awake. I like to see her before she goes to bed but it's not always possible with my irregular hours of work.'

'Saskia?' Anna asked.

'My daughter.' Jack gave her a quick glance. 'Didn't I mention her? I suppose I was too busy boring you with stories of my misspent youth.'

Anna felt stung. 'You didn't bore me!' Was her disinterest so obvious to him? And now, just as he was about to take her home, he mentioned that he had a child! She would have found that a much more interesting topic of conversation than hearing all about Anneka-the-party-girl.

'Tell me about Saskia,' coaxed Anna. 'How old is she?'

'Three. She had her birthday last week...we had a little tea-party for her.'

'We?' All of a sudden she was finding the conversation intriguing.

'There was Christine, my housekeeper-cum-nanny, Saskia's three little chums from nursery school and my parents, who came up from Cornwall. And I managed to make it through the whole party without getting called in to the hospital.'

'Sounds fun, the party,' said Anna. 'I've got three nephews and two nieces and I adored helping out at their birthday parties when they were small... Oh, you turn left here and my road is immediately on the right,' she instructed. 'I live in the block of flats near the postbox.'

Jack followed her directions and pulled to a stop outside her flat. He ran his eyes over her but this time they had a softer look, not the unsettling scrutiny that he'd been giving her ever since they'd met.

'Do you like children?' he asked.

'Very much,' she replied, reaching for the door-handle. 'Anyway, Jack, thanks for the drink.'

He saw her to the front door and then walked back to his car.

'See you at the hospital,' he called to her retreating back.

Jack drove home via the supermarket and picked up the strawberry yoghurt. When he arrived at his house he was told that Saskia was already in bed and asleep.

He'd been hoping that Christine might have kept her up after her bath, as she often did, so that he could see his daughter and put her to bed himself. He liked reading bedtime stories to her and asking what she'd done during the day. It was for him one of the highlights of the day.

'I thought you'd probably be home late,' said Christine, 'with you going out with a colleague.' He noted the hint of criticism in her voice.

He couldn't remember whether he'd mentioned that it was a female work colleague—but from the disapproving way she was reacting he guessed that he must have let slip that it had been a woman he was meeting. Christine, wonderful nanny and housekeeper that she was, was also overly protective of her employer. She was always warning him about 'unscrupulous women'—according to her, there were hordes of them who were just waiting to grab someone like him and trick him into marriage. If there *were* women throwing themselves at him, Jack had been too grief-stricken or too busy to notice. In fact, Anna Craven was the first woman he'd asked out since his wife died.

He went upstairs and crept into his daughter's room. He could see in the soft glow from her nightlight that she was asleep. He knelt by the side of her small bed and moved the teddy bear that was pressed up against her chubby cheek. She stirred slightly before resuming her blissful slumber. Her rounded features were still those of a baby even though she proudly told everyone that she was a 'big girl' now that she was three.

He touched her golden hair, stroking it gently with

his fingers. Her mother's golden hair...the mother she'd never known.

'Saskia,' he whispered softly, 'Sweet dreams, my darling.'

He gazed at her silently for several minutes, conscious of the almost imperceptible rise and fall of her breathing, watching over her like a guardian angel.

What a strange couple of days it had been! Days of such contrasting emotions. Yesterday, when he'd first seen Anna, the shock had almost felled him. He truly had thought he'd been starting to hallucinate...the pain he'd experienced had almost been physical in its intensity. Three years had been swept away in the blink of an eye when he'd come face to face with Anneka's double. Anneka, his adored wife, taken from him so suddenly and so cruelly.

Jack sighed deeply. Thank goodness for work, he mused. It had given him something other than his bereavement to focus on. And, later that day, when he'd found himself working with Anna, he'd been able to put the whole episode in perspective. He now realised that, apart from the close physical resemblance, Dr Anna Craven was very different from his late wife. He was so glad she'd agreed to go out with him for a drink—especially as she was the only woman he'd found remotely attractive in the last three years. Asking her out tonight had helped him to get over yet another obstacle as he clawed his way back to emotional normality. It hadn't been easy...to other men it would have been just a quick drink after work, but for Jack it had constantly brought back memories of happier times. There had been a time when he hadn't been able to imagine ever wanting to go out with another woman—but today he'd desperately wanted Anna to come out with him. Furthermore, he'd found her attractive. Extremely attractive.

'Welcome back to the land of the living,' he murmured to himself, still gazing fondly at his daughter.

Then he kissed her softly on the forehead, placed the teddy bear at the end of the bed and let himself out of the room, closing the door silently behind him.

CHAPTER TWO

THE following week, Anna changed from the day shift to the night shift. Although it played havoc with her sleep pattern, in some ways she preferred the night shift. The atmosphere in the hospital was completely different—a strange mixture of cosiness and danger.

During the long hours of the night shift, Anna was frequently reminded of why she'd chosen to specialise in A and E. It made her feel as if she was right in the centre of everything, with her finger on the pulse of life.

As she strode through the swing doors that led into the accident and emergency department, a small knot of tension formed in her stomach. It happened every time, particularly when she was on the night shift. She knew it would only be temporary and would disappear within a couple of minutes. It told her that the adrenalin rush had begun and that she was ready to swing into action without a moment's delay.

She hadn't taken more than a dozen steps when one of the nurses grabbed her.

'Dr Craven, you're needed in Resus One,' she said. 'Patient just admitted...young child...rescued from a house fire...extensive burns to his legs. Mr Harvey is in charge.'

She put on a sterile gown and walked briskly towards the resuscitation room. A light over the entrance was signalling a code blue. She quickened her pace. A code blue meant that a life-threatening crisis was on hand.

Resus One was a hive of activity. Several people in theatre blues and surgical gowns were circling the trolley and on it was the small, motionless figure of a child. The bottom half of his body was covered with the special wet dressings used for burns. Through the antiseptic-smelling air drifted another smell, the nauseating, never-to-be-forgotten smell of burnt flesh.

Jack looked up. Once again he experienced a chilling moment as the woman who so resembled his late wife walked into the resus room.

'Glad to have your assistance, Dr Craven,' he said, keeping his voice on an even keel, though his heartbeat had gone into overdrive. He'd get used to it, he told himself, working with her on a daily basis—and the shock waves would become less each time they met. Or maybe not...because these particular shock waves were becoming very pleasurable, he had to admit.

'We're prepping this young patent for a transfusion,' he told her. 'The burns are so bad that he needs blood as soon as possible or there's a good chance he'll die of shock.'

'What's his blood pressure?' she asked.

'Eighty over sixty,' a nurse replied. 'He's showing signs of shock.'

'How old is he?'

'About six, we think,' replied Jack. 'We don't know for sure because he was alone in the house when the fire started. His parents haven't been contacted yet.' He gave this information factually but Anna could see the rage in his eyes.

At that moment, the monitors surrounding the boy

began to bleep erratically as the lines on the screens became jagged and irregular.

'Get the defibrillator over here,' Jack shouted. 'He's arrested!'

Anna and the rest of the team went to work. The boy's oxygen level was increased and Anna moved forward, holding the defibrillator paddles.

'One, two, three—clear!' she called. Down went the paddles onto the boy's chest. There was a loud buzzing and the boy's small body was practically lifted off the operating trolley.

Everyone turned their attention to the monitor. The boy's heart was beating regularly again but the rate was weak, the green lines barely moving up and down.

'I think you should try again,' said Jack. 'Two hundred and forty joules again.'

Anna recharged the paddles and waited.

'One, two, three—clear!' she called, before again applying the defibrillator.

The team waited anxiously, all eyes on the monitor as the oxygen mask was clamped over the boy's face. The green lines on the screen settled into a regular rhythm, this time stronger than before.

'He's stabilising,' said Jack. 'Good. Keep the oxygen at ninety-five per cent. Well done, everyone!'

He looked at Anna as he said this. He would have liked to have said more. He'd have liked to have said, *You are terrific, Dr Craven, one of the best registrars I've ever worked with.* But instead he just kept on looking at her, his eyes dancing—and even though he was wearing a surgical mask she must have known he was smiling at her.

Now that they'd stabilised the boy's heart, the team

turned their attention to his legs. Jack gently pulled back the wet dressings, revealing the young boy's mottled, bleeding legs which had pieces of charred material stuck to them. The smell of burnt flesh intensified. But while his legs were very badly burned, the rest of his small body was mainly unaffected.

'He must have been wearing just pyjama bottoms,' said Jack as he set up the line for the blood transfusion, 'and they must have been made of untreated cotton. That's why they burst into flame with such tragic results.'

A nurse wheeled an intravenous pole across the room to the head of the trolley. 'I thought pyjamas had to be made of flame-retardant material,' she said. 'I thought it was the law.'

'It is,' said Jack bitterly, 'but this kid's pyjamas were certainly not flame-retardant. Any news of his parents yet?' He looked towards the door but no one was waiting outside.

'I'll go and find out, shall I?' asked Tammy, one of the nurses whom Anna recognised from the triage desk—the reception area where patients were sorted into categories depending on medical priority.

'Yes, please,' said Jack. 'There may be decisions to make about operating and we may need parental permission. Though what kind of parents must they be? People who leave a young kid alone in a house at night, while they, most likely, go out on the town! The police have been informed, I do know that.'

He watched as the first bag of blood was hooked onto the intravenous pole and the line attached to the patient. 'Now we need to set up the intravenous antibiotics,' he instructed.

Jack and Anna worked together smoothly and silently, each anticipating the other's actions. He was good to work with, Anna thought. He was quick and efficient and he exuded a calmness and confidence that she found mentally stimulating and physically reassuring. He was the ideal surgeon for the kind of situations they constantly faced in A and E.

'I wasn't expecting to find you on the night shift,' she said.

'I'm not,' he said wryly. 'I'm on the day shift but was asked to stay on when we got the call from the emergency services.'

Tammy came back into the resuscitation room, followed by a distraught man.

'This is the boy's father,' she said.

'How's my son? How's Jamie?' he asked anxiously. The medical team parted slightly, leaving a small gap through which the boy's father was confronted by the gory sight on the surgical trolley.

'Oh, my God!' he said. 'He's not dead, is he? Tell me he isn't dead!'

'He's alive but he isn't out of danger by any means,' said Jack, not wishing to soften the blow. His eyes were blazing. He was so mad that he wanted to put his blood-stained hands round the throat of the man who had allowed this to happen.

'I feel it's my fault!' said the man, running a hand through his tousled hair.

'I would imagine it *is* your fault,' Jack shot back, 'leaving a child as young as this on his own.'

'But it was only meant to be for a few minutes!' said the man wretchedly. 'I had to go—I had to take my wife to the hospital! She's eight months pregnant and she was bleeding and—'

'I thought I recognised you,' interrupted Tammy.

'I remember you coming in with your wife earlier in the evening. You're Mr Wyatt, aren't you?'

'Yes,' he confirmed. 'Todd Wyatt.'

'Well, Mr Wyatt, why didn't you call an ambulance?' Jack asked him, his anger barely concealed below the surface.

'I did, but it didn't come! I thought my wife was going to die. I went upstairs to Jamie's room and he was asleep. I thought I'd better not wake him up and bring him along with us because there was all this blood and everything. I thought it would really upset him. So when the ambulance didn't come I decided to drive her to hospital myself, thinking it would only take a few minutes, but the car broke down on the way back. When I finally got home the whole place was in flames, fire-engines everywhere.'

He put his hands over his face and sobbed. 'It was terrible! I thought Jamie was still in the house!'

Anna stripped off her latex gloves and binned them before putting a comforting hand on Todd Wyatt's shoulder.

'We hope it's going to be all right, Mr Wyatt. Your son's heart stopped at one point but he's stabilised now. He's been very badly burned and we're now sending him to the hospital's burns unit. They can do miraculous things these days with skin grafts. What happened to your wife? How is she?'

It was as though the man had completely forgotten about her for the moment.

'Oh,' he said, trying to cast his mind back to his other, earlier traumatic event. 'They've taken her in for observation. The baby might be born prematurely, they said. I'll go and check on her when I know what's going to happen with Jamie. I'll have to tell her, of course. Oh, hell, *how* am I going to tell her?'

'I'd like to talk to you about Jamie's pyjamas,' said Jack, still extremely angry with the man but accepting that he had been placed in a terrible dilemma.

'Pyjamas?' said the man, still in a state of shock. 'I don't know anything about pyjamas.'

'One of the reasons Jamie got so badly burned was because he wasn't wearing flame-retardant pyjamas. They're the only kind they're supposed to sell for children. It's the law.'

'I think he'd gone to bed in his new judo outfit, or just the bottom half of it. He was very chuffed with it, wanted to wear it all the time. My wife made it for him from some material she got from the market, you know, to save money. She's very clever with the sewing machine.'

Jack caught Anna's eye. 'Not so very clever, as it turned out,' he said under his breath.

The trolley, with Jamie on it, was in the process of being transferred to the burns unit.

'Tammy,' said Anna to the nurse, 'would you help Mr Wyatt find out what's happened to his wife?' Turning to the distraught man, she said, 'Jamie's condition is under control now. He's sedated and he's in good hands, and he won't really know whether you're here or not, Mr Wyatt, so you may as well go and be with your wife, particularly if they're delivering the baby. I'm sure you'll want to be there to give her support.'

Todd Wyatt followed the nurse to the main desk area and she sat him down while she made enquiries from the maternity unit.

Anna and Jack went into the changing room where they removed their surgical gowns, masks and hats.

'I must have a shower before I even *think* of going home, I'm so hot and sticky,' he said, reaching for a clean towel from the overhead lockers. 'You look as fresh as a daisy,' he said to Anna, his body very close to hers. 'It's always the way with the shift hand-over. The freshly laundered taking over from the jaded, perspiring ones!'

As he stretched up and grabbed the fluffy white towel provided by the hospital laundry, the heady scent of fresh, male sweat invaded her nostrils.

She was a fastidious person. Normally she couldn't stand being too close to a sweaty person—man or woman. But she didn't find Jack's glowing proximity at all repellent. Far from it. She amazed herself by actually finding it quite attractive. She breathed in again and almost felt like swooning. Must be something to do with pheromones, she thought with an inward laugh...although she'd always believed those special sexual chemicals were reserved for the animal kingdom—in particular, moths! She found herself laughing out loud.

'What's so funny?' he asked.

'I was just thinking about moths,' she said, then, moving away, added, 'It's too complicated to explain.'

'Do you like Mozart?' he asked.

She puzzled over the connection between moths and Mozart.

'Give up,' she said. 'I know he wrote something about a bat, *Die Fledermaus?* Or was that another composer?'

Jack leaned on the metal doors of the locker, his

body relaxed, all the tension from his long working day vanished. Her misunderstanding appeared to amuse him greatly.

'Forget moths,' he said, grinning at her. 'I'm talking about a Mozart concert at the Bridgemore Hall. Do you fancy coming along?'

Anna was about to refuse. Her mouth opened, but before she could get the words out he was one jump ahead.

'I've checked your rota. The concert's next week when you're on the day shift.'

'You checked my rota?' She wasn't sure whether to be flattered or annoyed at this evidence of snooping on his part. When he nodded, all she could bring herself to say was, 'Oh.'

'Do you like Mozart?' he repeated. 'When I mentioned loud disco music the other day you implied that your taste ran more along classical lines. And the tape I was playing in the car on the way to the pub was a Mozart symphony. You said you liked it...so I thought it would be nice to go to a live concert.'

He'd certainly done his homework!

'Well, I...' began Anna.

He'd put her in an awkward position. She liked him, and she was even beginning to find herself physically attracted to him, but she wasn't ready to start dating anyone at the moment. And yet it was going to be very difficult to turn him down, particularly when he said, 'I do hope you'll come, Anna. I haven't been out to a concert or a movie, or anything really, since I lost my wife. Going out on your own can be a very depressing activity in those circumstances.'

'I'm sure you could have found someone to go with

you,' she exclaimed, before realising how crass it sounded. She bit her lip.

'I'm sure I could,' said Jack. 'But that's not the point. I haven't *wanted* to ask anyone to come with me up to now. That's the difference. But if you don't like Mozart, I'll give the tickets to Christine and she can take a friend along.'

'Oh, but I *do* like Mozart,' said Anna, who was beginning to feel this conversation was leading in one direction only. Jack was so determined that she would go out with him that she might as well give in gracefully.

'What day is the concert?' she asked.

'Thursday,' he said.

'I'd love to come, Jack. Thank you very much. Now, you'd better take that shower and I'd better get back on duty.'

The next day, when she got back home after the night shift, there was a message on her answering machine.

'Hi, Anna, it's Rebecca. Give me a ring soon as you can, will you, darling? Bye for now.'

It was the only message waiting for her and, even though she was desperate for a hot bath and a lie-down, she decided she'd better phone her older sister straight away and get it over with. Rebecca didn't phone her all that frequently and she wondered if it could be something urgent, some family crisis perhaps? The tone of voice on the answering machine gave nothing away but then it never did as far as Rebecca was concerned. Her sister's 'telephone voice' was always the same—bossy, assertive and with a touch of false jollity.

She picked up the phone and dialled her sister's number.

'Thanks for ringing back,' said Rebecca at the other end. 'I thought you might have been at the hospital or on call or something.'

'I've just come off the night shift,' she said.

'Oh, good, then we can chat.'

'I'm very tired, Rebecca. Was there something special you phoned about? Otherwise I'd rather chat to you when I've had a bath and some sleep.'

'I won't keep you long, *Doctor*,' said Rebecca, who reacted as if she'd been rebuked. 'It's about the Gypsies...about Dad, really.'

Rebecca had always referred to their parents as 'the Gypsies' ever since their father had retired, sold the large family home and bought a small apartment and a top-of-the-range motor home. Their parents now spent a good part of the year travelling around Europe.

'What about Dad?' queried Anna. 'He's not ill, is he?'

'Good heavens, no!' replied Rebecca. 'I was talking to Jennifer and we were saying that as it's Dad's sixtieth birthday soon we should be thinking of having some sort of celebration. It's only a few weeks away and they're planning to be back in England for it.'

'Yes, you're right,' said Anna, her heart sinking at the thought of all the arrangements that would have to be made. 'We ought to do something for him, but what?'

'A party, of course,' replied her sister. 'That's why I phoned. I've arranged to have a meeting with

Jennifer one day next week so that we can discuss it. What about Thursday?'

The day rang a bell with Anna. She knew she wasn't on night shift...but...oh, yes, that was the day she'd agreed to go out with Jack.

'Can't do Thursday, I'm going to a concert,' she blurted out, before realising what she'd said.

'That's nice,' said Rebecca. 'With a man?'

Anna could visualise her sister's antennae whizzing round like mad, hoping to pick up any signals regarding her closely guarded private life.

'Yes,' she admitted. She was too tired and too mentally exhausted to attempt to head her off.

'You must tell us all about him when we have the meeting,' said Rebecca gleefully. 'Let's make it Friday instead of Thursday—eight o'clock at my house. Yes?'

'OK,' said Anna wearily.

The concert was wonderful. In fact, the whole evening was magical. It was for Anna the turning point in her recovery from her broken heart. Not once during the Mozart evening did she give a single thought to Liam.

She settled down in her seat and gave herself up completely to the experience. As the lights were raised at the end of the concert and the hall resounded with applause, applause that seemed never-ending, she felt as if she'd been reborn and was now able to start her emotional life once again. The heart-wrenching misery of the past weeks had vanished—thanks to Mozart. And thanks to Jack, too, she admitted. She came across him a lot at work—they always seemed to bump into each other at some point during the day. She found herself looking forward to catching a glimpse of him, however fleeting.

After the concert they went to a nearby Italian restaurant for a meal.

Anna chose *agnello con fagioli*—braised lamb with cannelini beans—and a green salad.

'Sounds good,' said Jack. 'I'll have the same.'

Sitting across the table from him, she was able to study him closely in a way she'd never previously done. His hair was very thick and vital-looking, even though it was clipped quite short. He was wearing a dark grey suit and the formality of it suited him. He was the kind of man, she judged, who'd look good in anything. Or nothing. As the thought entered her head she began, briefly, to fantasise about him naked. She felt herself colouring and banished the image from her mind.

'How's Saskia?' she asked.

'Fine,' Jack replied. 'She brought a picture home from nursery school today. One that she'd painted herself. It was of me, she said.'

'Is it a good likeness?' Anna smiled, imagining how the picture would look—probably a large, round head and stick-like arms and legs—the kind of paintings that three-year-olds did when trying to draw their parents. Rebecca and Jennifer used to have similar pictures stuck up all over their kitchen walls.

'I think it's a pretty good likeness, actually,' said Jack. 'You'll have to tell me what you think of it when you see it.'

Anna looked away. How was she going to handle this developing relationship? For a start, did she want it to develop into anything at all? If she wasn't careful she would get swept along and before she knew it she and Jack would be an item. She shivered slightly at the thought. She just wasn't sure if that was what she wanted.

They were halfway through their meal when he said, 'So who is he, this man who hurt you?'

Anna was taken aback. She had never mentioned Liam to Jack.

'What makes you think that?' she asked, giving nothing away.

He reached out and stroked the back of her hand with his long fingers. 'I don't need to be told. You've got it written all over your face. You look like a woman who's been hurt...emotionally. Am I right?'

She stared at him blankly. That evening, for the first time, she'd managed to put all thoughts of Liam out of her mind. Why did Jack have to start talking about him? What business was it of his?

When she didn't reply he continued stroking her hand, gently. He wrapped his fingers around hers, his eyes never leaving her face.

'He must be crazy, that's all I can say.'

She looked at him unblinkingly. Then she said, 'Shall we have the cassata for dessert?'

CHAPTER THREE

'THE first thing we have to decide is where we're holding the party,' said Rebecca. 'It can't be at the Gypsies' apartment because that's tiny.'

'Surely the first thing we have to decide is whether or not we're going to have a party for Dad. He may prefer *not* to have one,' suggested Anna.

'Nonsense,' snapped her sister. 'Of course he'll want a party!'

'I think Anna might have a point,' said her younger sister, Jennifer. 'Perhaps we could discuss the alternatives.'

The three sisters were seated round the gleaming white table in Rebecca's expensive new kitchen—a kitchen that had been designed by Jennifer's husband Neil. Anna felt that she had to make some comment about it or her sisters might imagine she hadn't noticed the transformation.

'Nice kitchen,' she said, looking round the gleaming new units and appliances. 'Of course, there was nothing much wrong with your old one, but this one is certainly impressive. Neil did a good job.' Anna hoped she'd used the correct phrases in praising the new kitchen.

'The old one was so dated that I couldn't possibly have put up with it for a moment longer,' said Rebecca scornfully. 'Neil came up with this brilliant scheme in polished steel and white oak—and we just *had* to have it!'

'Is Ted happy with it?' asked Anna, knowing that Rebecca's husband would have been given very little choice in the matter.

'Of course he's happy with it! Anyway, let's not change the subject. We're here to talk about a party for Dad for his sixtieth.'

'Or something else,' Jennifer butted in. She was the youngest and still determined not to be railroaded by her older sisters, particularly Rebecca.

'Like what?' demanded Rebecca, tapping the end of her pencil on her notepad.

They discussed a variety of alternative suggestions proposed by Jennifer and Anna and after half an hour they decided on a party. Anna had known that Rebecca would get her own way in the end and that it was a waste of time even mentioning anything else—but she also knew that Jennifer wouldn't be happy unless she'd made some sort of attempt to get her ideas through. Once again, Anna felt like the one in the middle...the peacemaker...the calming influence.

'So, a party it is!' announced Rebecca in triumph. 'Where shall we hold it?' She looked at the expectant faces of her two sisters. 'Would you like us to have it here?' She noticed the relief that momentarily flickered in their eyes. Of course they'd want her to hold the party there! Had a squirrel got a fluffy tail?

'Won't you find it a lot of trouble?' asked Anna, feeling slightly guilty. 'All the catering and everything?'

'We'll help,' said Jennifer quickly, anxious that her sister shouldn't change her mind. 'We'll do all sorts of baking and cooking, won't we, Anna?'

Anna's heart sank at the thought of baking and

cooking in her non-existent spare time. She needn't have worried.

'No problem,' assured Rebecca. 'We'll get caterers.'

'Should it be an evening or a lunch party?' Anna asked.

'Lunchtime,' said Rebecca without even hesitating. 'Dad will want his grandchildren there and I certainly couldn't cope with five tired and over-excited children whining all evening. The children will also be jolly useful at a lunch party. They can hand round sausage rolls and crisps and generally make themselves useful.'

Jennifer nodded in agreement. 'The twins would certainly enjoy that. Especially if your boys were here as well.'

Neil and Jennifer had five-year-old twin girls who hero-worshipped Ted and Rebecca's three boys who were aged ten, eight and six.

'Now, Anna,' said Rebecca, not wanting her sister to feel left out of all this family talk, 'tell us about this man you went out with yesterday. We want to know all about him. Is he a doctor like you?'

Anna's stomach clenched. She knew that Rebecca wouldn't have forgotten about her date the previous evening. It had just been a matter of when, not if, she'd mention it.

'He's a consultant at the Royal,' she said. 'He specialises in accident and emergency and that's where we met.'

Two pairs of hazel eyes were turned on her like beams from a car's headlights.

'And?' they asked together, expectantly.

'We went out to a concert last night. That's all

there is to it.' Anna took a gulp of the remains of her coffee. It was cold, but drinkable.

'Anna Craven, you are infuriating,' said Rebecca. 'Jennifer and I talk about our husbands and our previous boyfriends and all sorts of interesting things like that! Why can't you be the same as us?'

'Because I'm not,' said Anna, groaning inwardly.

'This is the first man you've mentioned for months,' said Jennifer. 'Rebecca and I were only saying that you didn't seem to have had a boyfriend for ages and ages. We decided it was because you work too hard.'

'I did have a boyfriend until quite recently,' she said, deciding to throw them a few stale morsels of gossip.

'You never said!' exclaimed Jennifer. 'So who was he and what happened? Was he also a doctor?'

'No, he wasn't. He was a bastard.'

Their mouths fell open at her vehemence. 'Language, Anna!' said Rebecca in mock horror.

'I went out with him for six months, he broke my heart and now it's all over. That's all I'm going to say. I'll have another cup of coffee, please.'

The brief outline information about Anna's former boyfriend appeared to satisfy her sisters' curiosity. It was more than they normally got out of her. A look of triumph crossed their faces as Jennifer held the cup for Rebecca to pour Anna fresh coffee.

Before the meeting finished they opened up their diaries and fixed a date for the party—a Sunday lunchtime—which was, conveniently, their father's actual birthday. As she left her sister's house to drive home, Anna felt a little triumphant herself. By telling her sisters the ancient history of her relationship with

Liam, she'd headed them off at the pass. They'd completely forgotten about the new man in her life—which was how Anna was beginning to think of Jack. The new man in her life!

She sighed contentedly as she drove home. Only a few more hours and she'd be seeing him again! Yesterday, as he'd dropped her home after the concert, he'd asked her out again. He'd kissed her and then walked her to her front door—where he'd kissed her again. As he'd held her body close, a languorous warmth had flooded through her. Then he'd gone, walking briskly back to his car and driving away the moment he'd seen her go safely through the door.

Anna had appreciated that he'd seemed to sense that she was unsure about inviting him in for a coffee or a nightcap. The fact that he hadn't tried to push his luck, as some others might have done, made her appreciate him all the more. He was as sensitive as he was sexy and for Anna that was a winning combination. And he could kiss for Britain! Her lips were still tingling at the memory of those two blissful kisses. She tried to recall what it had been like kissing Liam but for the life of her she couldn't remember! One thing was for sure—she was definitely over her former boyfriend, hence the way she was able to talk about him to her sisters.

The following day, Saturday, Anna wasn't rostered to work and so she didn't need to go in to the hospital—but she was on call. She'd arranged to go to the movies with Jack when her on-call hours had finished. She pottered about in the flat, doing all the household chores she never got time to do during her working week. She'd just put a load of sheets and towels into the washing machine when she got a call from the hospital.

'Road traffic accident,' said the duty nurse. 'Three cars involved, eight passengers, three badly hurt. We need you here, Dr Craven.'

When she arrived at the A and E she was directed to Resus Two where an injured woman was being attended by a junior doctor and two nurses. The young doctor was relieved when Anna took over the patient. He gave the verbal history.

'Middle-aged woman, multiple fractures to both femurs, massive blood loss. We're transfusing her with O-neg—no time to do a blood match. Her breathing's shallow, pulse weak.'

As Anna attended to her patient she asked, 'What about the other casualties? I heard there were eight people in the crash, three of them badly injured.'

'Dr Harvey is in Resus One with one of them—a man with a suspected ruptured spleen. The other patient was in Resus Three...had a fatal heart attack on the table. Of the five other people brought in, three children and two adults, most have only minor wounds and abrasions. They're being seen to by the nurses and a junior doctor.'

When Anna and her team had stabilised the woman with the multiple leg injuries and sent her up to Theatre in the care of the orthopaedic registrar, she went into Resus One to see if she could be of assistance to Jack.

Jack turned round momentarily.

'Hi, Anna. I could do with another pair of hands. Could you transfuse some O-neg and monitor fluids? We've sedated the patient because he was in tremendous pain. He had a large swelling on his abdomen.

We suspect a ruptured spleen. I'm preparing him for emergency surgery because if it is a ruptured spleen we'll have to send him to Theatre straight away. Theatre and the surgical team have been alerted. I think a surgeon is coming down to take a look.'

Anna got straight to work, hooking the bagged units onto the transfusion pole and finding a suitable point on the patient's arm to insert the lead. She was concentrating so hard that it was only when she'd secured the line that she glanced up at the patient's face. She gave a short gasp and continued staring at the lifeless body on the trolley. 'I know him! He's my brother-in-law, Ted Jarvis.'

Jack looked up in surprise. 'Well, if you'd rather not be involved, being a relative, I'll call for other assistance.'

Anna shook her head. 'You need me—there's nobody else available. The resus rooms are all busy.'

Mr Taylor, the surgeon, arrived and Jack apprised him of the situation. 'We haven't a moment to lose,' he said. 'We need to assess how bad the injury is—exactly what the problem is—and then get him up to surgery as quickly as we can.'

Mr Taylor quickly put on some latex gloves then looked at the swollen abdomen and felt the area gently. He looked up at the blood-pressure monitor and saw that Ted's blood pressure was dropping rapidly. 'I think you're right. It's probably a badly ruptured spleen, but we won't know until we open him up. The sooner, the better.'

'By the way, the patient is Dr Craven's brother-in-law,' Jack said, indicating Anna.

The surgeon looked up in interest. 'Do you happen to know his blood group?'

'No, I'm sorry, I don't,' she replied. 'We've been transfusing O-neg.'

'OK, we'll stick to the O-neg. Let's take him up. We'll try to repair it—but spleens are notoriously difficult to repair, even a surgeon of my skill,' he said, giving Anna an arrogant wink.

As the team wheeled the trolley towards the lift, a dreadful thought occurred to Anna. Had her sister been in the car with Ted? And if so, what had happened to her? She didn't know why she hadn't thought about it before, possibly because she'd been so engrossed in helping to save Ted's life.

'The patient who died in one of the other resuscitation rooms...the myocardial infarction,' she said, hardly daring to ask, 'was it a man or a woman?'

'Don't know,' Jack said, removing his surgical gloves.

'I need to know,' said Anna. 'I need to know if it was my sister because she might have been in the car with Ted.'

Jack reacted immediately. 'Will someone go and find out, please? As quickly as possible,' he instructed.

'I'll go,' said one of the nurses.

'Thanks,' said Anna, directing her gratitude towards Jack.

The nurse who'd volunteered to find out about the heart-attack victim was gone for a few minutes before returning and telling Anna that the patient was male; at the same time Rebecca came bursting into A and E in a state bordering on hysteria.

'What's happened?' she called out to the girl behind the triage desk. 'What's happened to my husband? The police have just been round to my house and said there's been an accident and—'

At that instant she saw Anna in her blood-splattered white coat holding Ted's designer loafers and his distinctive blue shirt. She let out a cry of distress.

'It's all right, Rebecca,' Anna assured her. 'Ted's in good hands. He's just gone up to Theatre. We think he's got a damaged spleen. They may have to remove it.'

'They're going to remove his spleen!' She put her hands to her mouth to suppress another cry. 'That sounds dreadful. It sounds... I mean, isn't a spleen *important*?'

Anna could see that her sister was out of her depth and the small amount of information she'd been given, instead of reassuring her, had only served to worry her even more.

'You're correct, Mrs Jarvis, in saying that the spleen is important,' Jack said, 'but it becomes less important the older we get. The spleen removes and destroys worn-out red blood cells and helps fight infection. In the foetus the spleen is very important because it actually produces red blood cells. But after birth this function is taken over by the bone marrow. And by the time we're adult the functions of the spleen are mainly carried out by the lymphatic system and the liver.'

As Jack explained about the operation, Rebecca became visibly more relieved and much less agitated.

'How long will he be in hospital?' she asked.

'We don't know,' Jack replied. 'But if they do remove the spleen, it'll be about a week or ten days, depending on how well he heals.'

'Oh, that's all right, then!' said Rebecca, smiling

for the first time. 'We can go ahead with our plans,' she told Anna.

'Plans?' said Anna vaguely.

'The party...for the Gypsies!' said Rebecca, back to her old, bouncy self. 'I'd better go and tell the boys about their father and that the news isn't as bad as we dreaded it might be. I've got them waiting outside in the car park.'

'The boys!' said Anna. 'They weren't in the car with Ted, were they?'

'No, thank goodness,' said Rebecca. 'He was on his way to pick them up from their swimming lessons when it happened. I got the fright of my life when the police appeared at my door and told me about the accident. It had involved three cars, they said, *and* there'd been children in some of the cars. I nearly had a fit! Fortunately one of the boys rang from the swimming baths to demand to know why Ted hadn't picked them up! So I went and got them on the way to the hospital.'

As they watched Rebecca's retreating form, Jack grinned at Anna.

'Gypsies? She's giving a party for gypsies? What a very interesting and amazing family you are!'

'I can explain all about it,' she said, laughing because she realised how crazy it had sounded. Jack put up his hand.

'No, please, don't explain,' he said. 'I'd much prefer to let my imagination run wild. Just promise you'll invite me to the party!'

They were in the changing room stripping off their operating gowns and gloves when, out of the blue, Jack said, 'Are you doing anything tomorrow?'

Anna had to get her mind in gear. Tomorrow...Sunday...day off and hopefully no emergencies.

'Only the usual,' she said. 'Late lie-in, read the Sunday papers, listen to *The Archers*.'

'Would you like to come with us to the zoo?' he asked. 'I promise it won't interfere with your lie-in and radio listening. We're going early afternoon. It's a special treat for Saskia.'

Anna's eyes brightened. 'That would be lovely,' she told him. 'I haven't been to the zoo for years, not since I was a small child.' Then she hesitated. 'But won't Saskia mind if I tag along on her outing? She doesn't know me and might think I'm pushing in.'

'Far from it,' replied Jack. 'I've told her all about you and she's dying to meet you.'

Anna studied him warily. 'You've told your daughter all about me? What kind of things could you possibly tell a three-year-old that would make her want to meet me?'

'I told her that you were an exceptionally talented casualty doctor...and that you give parties for gypsies,' he said.

Anna laughed out loud. 'Fibber! You only heard about the Gypsies today!'

'So you'll come to the zoo?'

'I'd love to.'

'Great. We'll pick you up just after two,' said Jack. 'That should give you plenty of time to read even the thickest of Sunday papers.'

Anna beamed and caught her reflection in the mirror. She hadn't smiled so much in weeks. She must definitely be getting over Liam. Definitely.

* * *

Jack drove to Anna's apartment block the next day, feeling very happy.

Anna was ready and waiting when the doorbell rang. She stepped outside, locked the door and followed Jack to the car. In the back seat was a young child—Saskia, she presumed—and a dark-haired woman. Anna took a closer took at the woman and estimated that she was in her late thirties or early forties.

Anna sat in the front next to Jack. He introduced her to the two back-seat passengers. 'This is Saskia,' he said, 'and this is Christine. And this is Anna,' he said, swivelling to face the back seat.

Both said, 'Hello', Saskia more shyly than Christine.

'We're giving Christine a lift to her parents' house. It's on the way.'

'Mum's not been too well,' said Christine in explanation. 'Anyway, I hope you have a nice day at the zoo. I was going to come along as well but then Jack said, as you were coming, I might as well spend the day with Mum.'

Christine's tone of voice gave nothing away and Anna wasn't sure...but she wondered if there was perhaps a tiny bit of resentment in that last remark.

'It's very kind of you to let me come along, Saskia,' said Anna, turning towards the little girl. The child said nothing but just stared solemnly at Anna in that direct, unnerving way that small children did. She was taking in every detail of this strange new friend of Daddy's and would reply when she was ready to do so!

The adults carried on talking and it wasn't long

before they pulled up outside Christine's parents' house.

Christine got out of the car.

'Thanks for the lift,' she said to Jack. 'I'll make my own way back so you needn't pick me up.'

'I hope your mother's no worse,' said Jack. 'Give her my regards, won't you?'

'I will,' said Christine. Then, looking from Jack to Anna, the smile vanished from her face. All she could think of was the life-size poster of Jack's first wife that he'd pinned on Saskia's bedroom wall. The likeness between the Anneka and this new 'girlfriend' was remarkable.

'Remarkable,' she said to herself, before realising she'd spoken her thoughts out loud.

As they drove away in the direction of the zoo, Anna asked Jack, 'What did Christine say just then? It sounded like "remarkable". Why would she say that?'

Jack slid his hand over hers for a brief second. 'If Christine thinks that you're remarkable after meeting you for such a short time, I can only presume she's psychic. I think you're pretty remarkable, too.'

'Daddy,' Saskia said in a piercing voice, 'can I take Fluffy to the zoo?'

'I'm not sure, darling,' said Jack. 'He might get eaten by a lion.'

'Who's Fluffy?' asked Anna.

'Her pet lamb. Not a real one! It's my daughter's favourite toy at the moment and it goes everywhere with her.'

'But I want to take him!' insisted Saskia, shaking the toy lamb in a determined manner.

'How big is he?' asked Anna, turning round to assess the size of the disputed toy. 'He might just squeeze into my handbag if you really want to take him. And then he'll be out of the sight of the lions. What does Daddy think?'

'Daddy thinks you'll be sorry,' muttered Jack under his breath. 'Fluffy will be in and out of your handbag like a yo-yo.' He grinned as he drove along, amused by how quickly his daughter had managed to twist Anna round her little finger.

When they arrived at the zoo, Saskia refused to sit in her pushchair.

'That's for babies,' she said assertively, clutching her toy lamb. 'I'm walking, holding Daddy's hand.'

'You might get tired,' said Jack. 'Shall we bring the pushchair just in case?'

'No!' said Saskia with firmness and finality.

They walked in the grounds of the zoo. Saskia was completely captivated by the animals, in particular the monkeys. Every now and then she would let go of Jack's hand and run excitedly up to the viewing area, dropping her toy lamb in the process. After Jack had picked it up for the umpteenth time he handed it to Anna, saying, 'Time to squeeze Fluffy into that handbag of yours. With a bit of luck she'll forget all about it.'

Anna surreptitiously hid the toy and she and Jack smiled conspiratorially at each other.

As he caught her eye, Jack realised with a jolt how very different she was from Anneka. The way Anna's smile lit up her entire face, her distinctive laugh and the way her eyes were so expressive even when she didn't utter a word. He marvelled that Anna and Anneka could, at first glance, have been so alike and yet utterly different. He was so pleased Anna had agreed to come on the outing today. As they passed other young couples with children, he enjoyed the secret sensation of knowing that he, Anna and Saskia must also seem like a 'real family' to onlookers.

Anna noticed him staring at her.

'What's the matter?' she asked. 'Have I got a smudge on my face?'

He paused for a minute and, taking her face in his hands, appeared to be scrutinising it inch by inch, touching her cheeks and eyebrows with his fingers, smoothing the palms of his hands across her forehead and chin and finally running one finger gently across her lips. Then he kissed her in all the places he'd touched.

'Perfect,' he said.

'Did I really have so many smudge marks on my face?' Anna asked suspiciously.

'Who said anything about smudge marks?' said Jack, a wicked glint in his eye. 'I just wanted to get my hands on you, Dr Craven, because I fancy you like mad.'

Anna laughed at the comical look on his face and, once again, Jack was reminded of how different she was from his late wife. How different—and how special.

They were interrupted by Saskia complaining that, even though she didn't want to go back for the pushchair, she was getting tired of walking. Jack ended up carrying her on his shoulders while she continued to shriek with delight at the elephants, lions and tigers.

They took a break for tea in the zoo café and Jack treated them all to sticky buns, milk shakes and ice cream. Saskia had decided by this time that she liked Anna very much and, at the end of the meal, she was the one who was allowed to lift her down from the chair to the floor. Anna was also allowed to wipe the crumbs of sticky bun and smudges of ice cream from her face.

'No, not you, Daddy,' she kept on saying whenever Jack attempted to do anything for her. 'I want Anna to do it!'

'We'll go and see the chimpanzees and the sea lions,' said Jack, 'and then it'll be time to be getting home. I don't think you want to see the reptile house, Saskia. It's just snakes and things like that.'

The little girl, her energy refreshed by the tea-break, jumped up and down clapping her hands. 'Snakes, snakes, I love snakes!'

'But you've never seen a real one, so how do you know?' said Jack quite reasonably.

'I *have* seen a snake!' insisted Saskia with complete certainty. 'I have a snake in my bedroom!'

'Goodness!' said Anna in mock horror. 'A *real* snake?'

'Yes,' said Saskia, nodding her head emphatically. 'It's a big, big, big snake and it sleeps in front of my bedroom door.'

'Goodness!' repeated Anna. She raised her eyebrows and said, as an aside, to Jack, 'And you say that my family's odd because we give parties for gypsies!'

Jack picked up Saskia and hugged her to him. 'You mean the draught-excluder snake, don't you? The one made from material.'

'It's still a snake!' said Saskia. 'So I want to see more snakes. Lots more!'

Jack turned to Anna. 'I trust you have no phobias about those particular creatures?'

She shook her head and giggled. 'No, but I'm not sure I want one in my bedroom!'

Jack's eyes twinkled with amusement. 'There are no snakes lying in front of my bedroom door,' he said as they walked in the direction of the reptile house, 'so you'd be perfectly safe in there.'

She didn't dare look at him—she didn't want him to see the heat rising in her face.

Saskia was getting tired and, as they'd seen nearly all the exciting animals the zoo had to offer, they set off for home.

'Are you picking up Christine?' Anna asked.

Jack shook his head. 'Her father's going to give her a lift or she'll get a taxi back, so she can stay to whatever time suits her,' replied Jack. 'Now, the thing is, shall I take you home now or would you like to come back and help me put Saskia to bed—and then take pot luck with something from the freezer? If Christine's back by the time you want to leave, I can drop you home—if she's not, I'll call a cab.'

'You seem to have all the alternatives worked out!' Anna said, laughing. 'Of course I'll come back and help with Saskia. I'm dying to see this snake for a start!'

Saskia enjoyed the extra attention at bathtime. Usually there was just Christine around, although Jack did sometimes come rushing home in time to read her a bedtime story. And sometimes he was the one who bathed her, but that wasn't very often.

She liked Anna because she put lots and lots of bubble stuff in the bath, whereas Christine and Daddy only used one capful.

'I've lost all my boats,' squealed Saskia with delight when the really deep bubbles hid her bathtime toys.

'All we have to do is put some soap in the water and all the bubbles will disappear and we can find your boats again,' said Anna.

'No!' said Saskia. 'Not yet! I like it like this.' And she thrashed around, kicking her chubby legs and pretending to swim.

'You seem to know an awful lot about bubbles,' said Jack, who was holding a fluffy bath towel for when Saskia decided she'd had enough.

'I've got five nephews and nieces, remember,' she said, grinning at him and tucking a strand of damp hair behind her ear.

'Come on, Saskia, I think it's time to get out of the bath now,' said Jack, holding out the towel.

'No!' she said, preparing to throw a tantrum.

'Right, Saskia,' said Anna, waving the bath soap, 'don't you think it's time we rescued all your boats? I bet you can't remember how many are lost in the bubbles, can you?'

'Yes, I can,' said Saskia, putting a thoughtful, bubble-coated finger to her cheek. 'Four,' she said. 'Four boats.'

'I think there are only three,' said Jack, winking at Anna.

'I think there are six,' said Anna, winking back. 'Shall we find out, Saskia? There's a prize for the winner.'

'What prize?' she asked suddenly, staring at Anna with big wide eyes.

'A prize of a big bottle of bubble bath,' said Anna.

'Where is it?' asked the child, looking around the bathroom.

'It's in the shop at the moment,' replied Anna keeping a straight face. 'The winner decides on what colour it's going to be...blue or yellow or red or green or pink.' Anna counted off the tempting list on her fingers.

'Pink!' said Saskia enthusiastically. 'I want pink!'

'We'll have to see if you've won it first,' said Jack.

'Oh, quick,' said Saskia. 'The soap, let's do the soap!'

Anna plunged the bar of soap into the bath and as she lathered it up the bubbles disappeared as if by magic. The four little boats hove into view.

'Hurrah!' said Saskia as she counted them and realised she was the winner. She stood up and put her arms out for Jack to lift her out of the bath and into the large towel.

'That's the quickest way I've seen yet of getting Saskia out of the bath. Left to herself, she'd sit in the bubbles till the water was stone cold.'

Anna pulled out the plug and rescued the bar of soap. 'The soap trick is quite a good one, isn't it? Of course, you may have to combine it with a bribe, like another bottle of bubbles, which, of course, I shall be buying on my next shopping trip!'

When Saskia was in her pyjamas and ready for bed, Jack asked her who she would like to read her a bedtime story.

'Both of you,' she said emphatically.

'We'll read one each,' said Jack, adding, 'Two short ones instead of one long one.'

'Two *long* ones,' insisted his daughter, who was an expert at getting her own way.

They sat by the side of her bed and Jack read the first story from one of her fairy story books. The room was very pretty—decorated and furnished to delight a small girl, with lots of shelves for her toys and books and a small dressing table and matching cupboards. By the side of the door was the famous snake—a long, round and softly padded draught excluder covered in a luridly patterned fabric with two pearly buttons for eyes.

As Jack read the story, Anna's eyes wandered around the room. On the wall opposite the small bed was a framed photograph, enlarged almost to poster size. Anna stared at it. It was like looking into a mirror.

This must be Anneka, she realised with a jolt. The likeness was emphasised by the almost identical hairstyle worn by the woman in the photograph. Anna moved her hand to her head and felt for the parting. Heavens, she thought, we even part our hair on the same side. A great sadness swept over her...not particularly for Jack, but for Saskia. The larger-than-life photograph dominated the room...it would be the last thing the little girl would see at night and the first thing she'd see on waking. And yet it was only a picture...and it was possibly all Saskia had as a reminder of her mother...and it brought a lump to Anna's throat.

After they'd each read a story, tucked Saskia up in bed with her favourite teddy and each kissed her goodnight several times, Saskia sighed and fell asleep almost immediately. They tiptoed out of the room and, leaving the door slightly ajar, went downstairs.

In the kitchen Jack began opening and shutting cupboard doors, peering in the fridge and the freezer.

'We've got lots of frozen meals for one,' he said, pulling out three or four boxes. 'Christine buys them by the dozen. She tends to eat her meals with Saskia, and as I'm never sure what time I'll be home this is what I normally have.'

Anna surveyed the selection he'd laid out on the scrubbed-pine table.

'There are two lasagnes,' she said. 'Let's have those. And we can make a salad to go with them. Have you any lettuce and tomatoes?'

He opened the fridge again and rummaged in the salad drawer. He pulled out a bag of ready-washed baby lettuce leaves, a bag of wild rocket and a packet of vine tomatoes.

'A feast for a king!' she said as they set about putting the meal together.

When the lasagne was cooked, they carried it into the living room where Jack had set up a small table and placed a candle in the middle. He produced a bottle of Chianti and two glasses. They sat down opposite each other, clinking their glasses together.

'Cheers,' said Jack. 'Thanks for coming with us today.'

'Thanks for asking me,' said Anna.

She meant it, she really did. She'd enjoyed herself more than she could say, playing happy families with Jack and his adorable little girl. Seeing him like this, away from the hospital environment, had brought a whole new dimension to how she felt about him. She'd always found him physically attractive, exceptionally so, and she greatly admired his medical skill...but now...now she found him more than attractive—she found him *lovable*. She wouldn't go so far as to say she was *in love* with him—but she was well on the way to falling for him.

Jack, too, was finding himself deeply attracted to Anna. The more he saw of her, the more he felt that this woman was something special, someone he wanted to be part of his life. He had truly never met anyone like her—and he was determined to give the relationship the best chance he could. There was just one cloud on the horizon as far as he could make out. He sensed that Anna had been very bruised emotionally by someone in the recent past. Was she still holding a candle for him? Could this mystery man put an end to any future plans that he might have for the two of them? It was early days, he knew that. But he needed to get things out in the open. If she was still in love with this former boyfriend, what chance was there for him? He gripped the stem of his wineglass, summoning up the courage to broach the subject.

'Would you mind if I asked you again about that man—the one who hurt you?' he said after a little while.

Anna felt herself going hot. She hadn't given Liam a thought for a long time and she didn't welcome talking about him now. But she realised she'd have to say something, especially as it had become obvious to Jack that she'd recently been hurt.

'I don't mind you asking,' she said, and as she spoke she realised that, no, she didn't mind at all. She didn't mind talking about Liam because now the pain was less raw.

Jack remained silent, just looking at her, his brown eyes studying her face, watching for any sign that she might still be hankering after her former lover.

Anna was touched to her soul by the intensity of

his gaze. He cared for her, that much was obvious, and he wanted to know if she felt the same or if there was another man who still owned the key to her heart.

'It's all over now,' she said calmly, 'but I was desperately unhappy at the time. His name was Liam, and foolishly I fell in love with him. But Liam was someone who was unable to make any commitment. He was charming, handsome...and a complete bastard.'

She paused for a moment, realising that she was much more able to talk openly about Liam—and her feelings towards him. Yet, having described Liam as a bastard, she also realised that she was only speaking the truth about what she felt and as a result she now felt a whole lot better about the break-up. That's what the truth does, she mused. It makes you free...free to love again.

She met Jack's gaze and in his eyes she imagined that she could see mutual understanding. He reached out and covered her hand with his, sending an electric charge rushing through her.

He stood up and moved towards her, raising her to her feet. Cupping her face in his hands, he stared at her for a brief moment, his eyes dark and brooding.

Then he bent over her and their mouths met softly, tenderly. He slid his arm around her body and pulled her close to him, kissing her with mounting desire. She responded with a surge of passionate need and, as his mouth moved hungrily against hers, she put her arms round his neck, her hands pushing into his dark hair, her whole body pressing against his.

The sound of the front door slamming split them apart. They sprang back, flushed and breathing heavily. Jack regained his composure and strode into the hall.

'How did you get back?' she heard him say.

He walked into the living room with Christine. Anna was gathering up the plates and glasses from their meal.

'Hello again,' she said to Christine, smiling brightly.

Christine acknowledged her with a curt nod before answering Jack's question.

'I got a taxi,' she said. 'I'll just slip my coat off and give you a hand with those dishes.'

'You needn't worry,' said Anna. 'I'll happily do them. There's no need for you to do it, Christine.'

'It's hardly a big deal whoever does it,' said Jack. 'There's a dishwasher in the kitchen.' He put out the candle with a flick of his hand, leaving just the side lights to illuminate the room.

The matronly Christine marched into the room again and swept the remaining items off the small table.

'Now that I'm back, you might as well give your friend a lift home,' she said to Jack in a voice that made Anna feel like a child.

Jack winked at Anna. 'Good idea,' he said. 'Perhaps we can have our coffee at your place?'

'Oh, I'm sorry!' said Christine. 'How rude of me! I hadn't realised that you'd not finished your meal. Please, allow me to make you both a coffee.'

But by then Jack and Anna were in the hall and on their way out.

'No, thanks, Christine,' called Jack. 'I'm sure Anna won't mind making me a cup of instant.'

* * *

'Weak or strong?' asked Anna, as they stood in the little kitchen of her flat, the spoon hovering over the coffee-jar.

'Medium,' said Jack, slipping his arms round her waist and making it almost impossible for her to get the coffee grains into the cups without spilling them. But neither of them cared.

She put down the spoon and turned into his embrace. His dark head came down and his mouth found hers for the second time that evening. This time their kiss was slower and less urgent, but it was just as passionate.

Her whole body arched against him as they kissed each other with a hungry intensity. His mouth explored hers deeply and her body melted into his, overcome by a mindless sensuality that made her forget any other man she'd ever kissed or loved. She knew that if he wanted to make love to her right there on the kitchen floor she wouldn't mind.

Anna Craven, normally so reserved and cool, was a seething mass of desires. But while she, uncharacteristically, appeared to have lost all inhibition, Jack was decidedly in control.

He knew exactly what he was doing. He wasn't going to spoil everything by acting like an opportunist. He was keen to get her into bed but he knew that if he did—so soon into their relationship and so quickly following her break-up with Liam—she might come to regret it. She might even consider that she'd been acting on the rebound—and he certainly didn't want that. Reluctantly, because he was also extremely aroused, he deliberately slowed the tempo down, taking some of the heat out of the fire. He kissed her cheek and cradled her head on his shoulder, moving his hand slowly down her hair—hair that was the colour of moonlight—stroking its silky length.

'I'll go without the coffee and just go home,' he said hoarsely.

'You know you can stay, don't you?' she whispered.

'Yes.'

Their mouths met again, softly and gently, in a kiss of quiet love.

'I hope you'll ask me back for coffee again some time soon,' he said, his words full of double meaning. He picked up his car keys and headed for the door. He blew her a kiss. 'Thanks again for coming to the zoo. You made Saskia's day.'

'Tell her I haven't forgotten about the pink bubble bath,' she replied, blowing a kiss back to him.

CHAPTER FOUR

'JUST call out as many names as you can think of and then we can trim the list down if necessary,' said Rebecca, pen and paper in hand.

The three sisters were meeting at Jennifer's house to work out the party details—who to invite, the kind of food they'd want and whether it should be a buffet or a sit-down lunch. First of all they were each supplying as many names of their parents' friends as they could remember.

'There's Roger and Marge, John and Ellie, Albert and June,' said Anna, reeling off the most obvious names. Rebecca wrote them down.

'What about Carole and Andy?' suggested Jennifer, 'and Greg and Sue?'

'I'll put them all down,' said Rebecca. 'I've added Cathy and Peter, and Todd and Maria. Anyone else?'

'Can't think of anyone else that we could describe as being Mum and Dad's close friends,' said Jennifer. 'Oh, what about Irene, that old school friend of Mum's? She got married again recently, she told me, to an airline pilot. I think his name is Bill.'

'How many does that make, including Irene and Bill?' asked Anna.

'Sixteen,' Rebecca replied. 'Then, of course, we have to add all of us...so there's me and Ted and our three, Jennifer and Neil and your two, and Anna.' She looked at her sister expectantly. 'Will you be bringing someone?' she asked.

'I think so,' replied Anna, smiling cautiously and hiding beneath a length of blonde hair that had fallen across her face. 'But he may not be available to come.'

Her sisters exchanged intrigued glances. She could almost hear their antennae working.

'Shall I write down a name,' asked Rebecca innocently, 'or are you keeping this mystery man as a surprise?'

Anna tossed her hair back over her shoulder and laughed lightly. 'He's no secret, I assure you. His name is Jack and he's no mystery man either. You've already met him, Rebecca.' Anna was amused to note how her sister's jaw had dropped. 'He's the A and E consultant who looked after Ted following the accident.'

Recognition spread over Rebecca's face.

'Then I'll look forward to meeting him in civvies,' she said. 'I can hardly remember much of what happened that day except my relief that Ted had survived the car crash.'

'How's Ted doing now that he's back home?' asked Anna.

'Absolutely fine. He's even managing to do a bit of office work at home—the doctor said it would be all right as long as it wasn't anything too stressful. It'll be a few weeks before he can drive again, so he won't be going back to work full time until then.'

'Are you sure you still want the party at your house? It won't be too much for Ted?' asked Anna. 'We could always hire a room in a hotel.'

'I wouldn't dream of it! Ted is already looking forward to having everyone at our place,' Rebecca assured them. 'Now, let's add up these numbers…I make it twenty-nine, including the Gypsies. So that probably means a buffet lunch rather than a sit-down meal. If the weather's nice we can have it in the garden—it's looking terrific at the moment.'

'What if it rains?' said Anna. 'This is England, remember.'

'We could put up one of those small marquees,' said Rebecca. 'Ted has a friend who rents them out. Ted's firm uses them a lot for business and trade functions—launches of new lingerie ranges and that kind of thing—so he'll no doubt let us have a small marquee for an even smaller fee, or maybe for nothing at all. He'll want to keep in with Ted, I'm sure.'

Rebecca's husband worked in the clothing industry. He was a director with special responsibility for ladies' underwear, or 'lingerie' as Rebecca insisted on calling it. The one guaranteed way to make her an enemy for life was to describe Ted, even jokingly, as 'being in ladies' underwear'—or, worse still, 'in ladies' knickers'.

'That's a good idea about the mini-marquees,' said Jennifer. 'You can get really pretty ones with green and white stripes.'

'Now for the catering. Any suggestions about who we should get?' asked Rebecca, pen poised.

'I'd have thought that was obvious!' said Jennifer, looking as if she was about to be offended. 'Neil's sister Liz would be wonderful. I told you about her, Rebecca. Dad's party is just the kind of thing she'd do to perfection.'

'I didn't know Liz was into catering,' said Anna, who, by choice, tended to miss out on much of the family gossip. 'Wasn't she recently divorced?'

'Indeed she was,' confirmed Jennifer. 'She's had a

really tough time and now she's trying to make a go of this catering business. She's put virtually all her divorce settlement money into the new venture, re-mortgaged her house, sold her car and bought a small van. Apart from the fact that she's a very good caterer, she really could do with the money—and the contacts she'll make at the party will do her no harm either. You know how word gets around.'

'Fine,' said Rebecca. 'We'll agree to give the catering job to Liz, shall we? Keep it in the family, so to speak.'

Her sisters nodded in agreement.

'Ask her to let us have some sample menus,' said Rebecca, 'and then we can decide on what to order. I presume she does everything, vegetarian as well as meaty things?'

Jennifer said she imagined Liz would, but she'd check just in case. She and Rebecca offered to write out all the invitations, knowing that Anna's time was limited.

'With a bit of luck we'll have everything organised and well in hand before the Gypsies arrive home next week,' said Rebecca.

She called the meeting officially to an end and Jennifer went to put the kettle on. As she walked past Anna she said, 'So, are you and this Jack an item?'

Anna hesitated, but only for a second. She felt so happy and confident about Jack that she didn't mind her sisters knowing about the two of them.

'Yes,' she said with a grin, 'I suppose you could say that.'

Jennifer patted her on the shoulder.

'Fabulous,' she said. 'I hope he's the marrying kind because my girls are just desperate to be bridesmaids.

And they're just at the right age to look absolutely adorable in matching "little bride" outfits.'

'Hang on, Jennifer,' said Rebecca, 'it's the real bride who's supposed to steal the show, not your five-year-old twins! But, seriously, Anna, my boys would look stunning in those miniature morning suits they have these days. Blue satin pageboy outfits with buckled shoes aren't the fashion any more, you know. But can't you just see our boys in those neat suits and fancy waistcoats that would be smaller but identical versions of Jack's morning suit?'

'With matching buttonholes, of course!' added Jennifer. 'Do they wear top hats at weddings these days?'

'Hey, slow down, you two.' Anna laughed at her sisters' enthusiasm. 'Jack and I have only been out on a few dates. We're a long way off booking the reception!'

'All I was saying,' repeated Jennifer, 'was that I hope he's the marrying kind. So many men aren't these days. Suddenly it's fashionable to have a "partner" and no wedding at all. Well, that's a bit of a disappointment, I always think. There's nothing to beat a really good wedding.'

'To answer your question,' said Anna, 'I think that Jack probably *is* the marrying kind—because he's already *been* married.'

'Oh,' said her sisters in unison.

'Does that mean he's divorced?' asked Jennifer.

Anna shook her head.

'You don't mean to tell me you're involved with a married man!' said Rebecca. '*You*, of all people, Anna! I would have thought you'd know better. It only leads to heartbreak—if not for you, then for the wife he's left behind. As your eldest sister, I feel it is my duty to warn you not to do anything you'll regret.'

'You can forget the lecture, Rebecca,' said Anna, holding her annoyance in check. Why did her sister always end up bossing her around? 'Jack is a widower. His wife died of a ruptured aneurysm soon after giving birth.'

'The poor man!' said a chastened Rebecca. 'And the baby, was that all right?'

'She's fine,' said Anna. 'She's called Saskia and she's just turned three.'

'There you are!' said Jennifer. 'Now you can have *three* little bridesmaids at your wedding!'

When Anna saw Jack at work the next day she asked him if he'd be able to come to the party.

'Is this the one for the gypsies?' he asked, checking the date in his diary.

'That's right.' Anna laughed. 'Would you like me to explain about it?'

'Perhaps you'd better,' he said. 'I'm writing it down as a firm date and I suppose I'd better find out what the dress code is. Is it Romany or vagabond?'

He stroked a finger down her cheek and brushed his lips briefly against hers, sending a charge of sexual excitement through her. Her skin bloomed with colour and warmth. He didn't seem to mind or care that other people were watching them. It was as if he wanted the world to know they were going out together.

'My sisters nicknamed my parents the Gypsies because now that Dad's retired they spend months travelling round Europe in a motor-home,' she explained.

'Not a horse-drawn caravan?' said Jack, putting on a long face. 'How disappointing.'

'Now that you come to mention it,' she said, 'they did once have a holiday in Ireland in a horse-drawn caravan. But that was years ago. This party is for Dad's sixtieth birthday. I'm glad you can come.'

'Barring emergencies, as always,' he said.

'Of course. But that applies to me as well. Let's keep our fingers crossed because it would be a good opportunity for you to meet my family. I've met yours...well, Saskia anyway. And she's the most important one.'

'She thinks you're pretty important, too,' said Jack, 'particularly after I took her that pink bubble bath you bought.'

'I'm glad she liked it. I hope it was the right shade of pink—I know how much that matters to little girls. I've learnt that much from my five-year-old nieces.'

'Will I meet them at the party?' asked Jack.

'Yes,' confirmed Anna, adding, 'Do you think Saskia would like to come along? It's mainly adults—all Dad's friends from years ago—but my sisters' children will be there.'

'Saskia would love it,' said Jack. 'Thank you.'

He watched her walk away, his eyes taking in every movement—the sway of her hips and the way her shapely legs brushed, very slightly, against each other. He hadn't noticed that before...and he found it incredibly sexy.

He strode after her and, taking her by the arm, said, 'There's just one more thing I meant to talk to you about.'

She looked slightly surprised as he steered her into

a nearby laundry room. A very small laundry room which was more of a walk-in cupboard.

Closing the door behind them, he said huskily, 'This is what I want to talk about.'

He was standing very close to her and Anna felt her pulse beat with sexual awareness. He lifted one hand and lightly stroked her throat, sliding his fingers under her hair and around the back of her neck. His other hand cupped her breast. Anna trembled at his touch. His hands were so gentle, their slow movements intensely seductive. She felt her flesh burning and her heart pounding as he lowered his head slowly until his lips touched hers, softly and sensually. The instant his mouth was on hers, his kiss turned into a kiss of fire. She responded hungrily, her fingers twisting in his thick, warm hair. He pushed her against a stack of folded sheets and towels, his body pressed up against hers as an intense passion took hold of both of them.

She'd never felt such physical and emotional attraction to any man. She was amazed, in those few stolen moments in the hospital laundry room, how much desire he had awakened in her. As his mouth closed over hers again and again, she returned his kisses with a fervour she'd not known she was capable of, never wanting the moment to end.

Was this what it felt like when you fell in love? She'd believed she'd been in love with Liam but this was in a whole new league. Was this love or was it just raw, sexual attraction? To hell with it, she thought. At that particular moment, with something that felt this good, did it matter anyway?

On the day of the party, Anna went round to Rebecca's a good hour before the guests had been asked to arrive. She was feeling a little guilty at having left most of the last-minute arrangements to her sisters—at their insistence.

'You'll be far too busy saving lives, darling,' said Jennifer, 'so don't you worry about anything else. Just turn up a little earlier than the guests and we can have a "family only" pre-party celebration for Dad. We can give him his presents and cards and that kind of thing.'

When she arrived she was relieved to see that everything was well under control, including the five children. They were all dressed in smart party clothes and were sitting in a close little group clustered around their grandfather, helping him open a stack of birthday cards and presents.

Anna went over and kissed him.

'Happy birthday, Dad,' she said, handing him her card and present. The twins were already ripping off the wrapping paper before her father had time to say thank you.

Her mother came into the room, looking stunning in a lemon-coloured silk suit. Mrs Craven was strikingly attractive and looked years younger than her age. Her hair, which at one time had been as dark as Rebecca's and Jennifer's, now was a lighter shade and was cut fashionably short and gleamed with sun-streaked highlights.

Both her parents looked tanned and fit after their two months away, touring France, Spain and Italy. Anna had spoken to them on the phone shortly after they'd arrived back but this was the first time she'd seen them. Her mother hugged her and then stood back to survey her daughter.

'I must say, Anna, you're looking terrific! That tiny skirt shows off your long legs to perfection. And the aquamarine top goes so well with your lovely blonde hair.'

'You're looking pretty fantastic yourself, Mum,' said Anna, giving her another squeeze.

Her mother had the knack of making the most blatant flattery sound sincere, leaving the recipient with a warm, feel-good glow. Even if Mrs Craven had heartily disapproved of her daughter's choice of outfit—Anna *had* wondered if the micro-skirt, tightly fitting top and bare midriff was possibly a *little* too revealing—she would never have dreamed of saying so. She was a mother who inspired confidence and self-belief in her daughters.

Her father had finally managed to get a look at Anna's card and present but not before they'd been handed round the group of children sitting at his feet.

'Thanks, Anna,' he said. 'How did you know I needed a new camera?'

'A little bird told me,' she said, winking at her mother. 'I hope it's the kind you like. If not, I can change it for you.'

'This is absolutely perfect,' he enthused, 'and it's got a built-in zoom. It's much better than the one that broke.'

Her mother spoke in a low voice to Anna. 'He means the one that he dropped on the stone floor of the Sistine Chapel!'

Rebecca and Jennifer came into the living room and greeted Anna.

'Won't you be a little cold in that?' asked Rebecca, looking with disapproval at Anna's bare midriff. 'Being a doctor, I'd have thought you'd want to dress more sensibly, just in case the weather turns breezy.'

Anna laughed. 'It's precisely because I'm a doctor and normally have to wear boringly practical clothes that I felt, for once, I'd dress a little daringly and to hell with the breeze!'

'Yes, darling,' said Jennifer, 'and, of course, being a doctor, you can always cure yourself if you *do* get pneumonia, for instance.'

Anna laughed again and, leaving them to their disapproval walked through to the kitchen. She wasn't going to let her sisters rile her. Not today when she was feeling so happy and relaxed. It was her father's birthday party and she was really looking forward to it...and she was particularly looking forward to introducing Jack and Saskia to her parents. She had a feeling that it would be a defining moment in their relationship—an important 'family moment'.

In the kitchen she met up with Liz, Jennifer's sister-in-law. Liz and a couple of assistants were bringing the food in from the van which had been parked close to the house.

'Everything looks under control,' said Anna, surveying a scene of calm and efficient organisation. Crates of prepared food were being unloaded onto every available surface.

'Are we having a cold buffet?' she asked. 'That would probably be the easiest.'

'Your sisters chose a bit of each,' said Liz. 'There'll be cold salmon and coronation chicken, a spicy beef curry, which is tasty rather than throat-burningly hot, and hot and cold vegetarian dishes.'

'It all sounds wonderful,' said Anna. 'It smells

lovely, too. Is that herb bread?' She pointed to a large bread basket on the kitchen table.

'Yes, coriander and garlic,' said Liz. 'We'll serve that slightly warmed. It makes an enormous difference to the flavours.'

In the garden Ted and Neil were inspecting one of the two mini-marquees that had been erected earlier that morning. Anna walked inside and joined her brothers-in-law. There were some smart-looking folding chairs which the two men were in the process of opening up and in the centre was a long table covered with a white damask cloth.

'This looks very good,' she said, wondering what else you could say about a tent.

The two men stopped what they were doing and Ted took the opportunity to sit down on one of the chairs. It was still early days in his recovery from his spleen operation and he tended to get tired very quickly.

'Hello, Anna,' he said.

'Yes, hi, there,' said Neil, running his eyes appreciatively over her skimpy outfit.

'What's in the other tent?' she asked. 'Is it the same as this?'

'Pretty much the same,' said Neil, 'except that it's where the caterers will be putting the food. All the plates and cutlery and everything will be laid out on that table. This table is just for people to come in and eat their food here if they want to, instead of in the garden.'

Anna looked out onto the garden again and noticed the half-dozen smaller tables covered with long, lacy tablecloths.

'I must say it all looks lovely,' she said in genuine

admiration, 'and the garden looks amazing. Ted, I hope you've not been doing it yourself? Lawnmowing is a bit too strenuous so soon after your op.'

'No fear,' he said. 'I've been using this garden maintenance company for a couple of years now, which, of course, was a godsend when I had the accident. It meant one less thing to worry about, keeping the garden tidy.'

The doors from the living room into the garden were open and Rebecca walked out onto the terrace. She called over to them, 'The guests will be arriving soon!'

Ted and Anna left Neil to finish opening up the chairs and followed Rebecca through into the house.

'Are you and Neil all sorted out about the drinks?' she asked her husband anxiously.

'Yes, Rebecca, don't panic. Everything's laid out in the dining room—and the champagne's in the fridge.'

The doorbell rang and as Rebecca went to see who it was, Jennifer and her mother hastily tidied away the last remnants of the torn wrapping paper.

It was Jack and Saskia.

'I had instructions to come a little early,' he said, looking past Rebecca and searching for Anna's face. When he saw her his heart skipped a beat. She looked stunning and, to his mind, the most beautiful woman in the world. She smiled at him—a warm, sexy smile—and at that moment he would have done anything for her.

'Jack,' she said, beckoning him in, 'you remember Rebecca, don't you? You operated on her husband.'

'Delighted to meet you again,' he said to Rebecca, 'and this time under happier circumstances.'

He followed Anna into the living room and was introduced to her parents and to Jennifer. He was holding Saskia firmly by the hand.

'This is my daughter, Saskia,' he told them. 'She can be a little shy at first,' he said, noticing how the little girl was clinging on to his leg with her other hand.

Saskia lost her shyness when the five-year-old twins came bounding into the room. She was then more than willing to let them carry her off to join in one of their games which they were playing with Rebecca's youngest son, Jasper, who was six.

Within a short time, the other guests started to arrive and everyone congregated in the garden. Neil and Ted were serving the drinks, assisted by Ted's two older boys, William and Richard, who, at ten and eight, felt too grown-up to be playing games with the little ones. Liz and her two assistants, smartly attired in white jackets and black trousers, handed round plates of delicious-looking canapés.

Two more guests arrived, the final ones, Irene and Bill Stone. Irene was the old school friend of Mrs Craven's who had recently married an airline pilot. He was, according to Mrs Craven, 'very dashing'. Anna had smiled at the old-fashioned description, imagining someone who was a cross between a matinée idol and a Second World War flying ace. When she saw him in the flesh she had to suppress a giggle because he turned out to be just as she'd imagined!

Jack, who was standing next to Anna when they were introduced to Irene and Bill, had a puzzled look on his face.

'You look very familiar,' he said, 'but I just can't

place where it is I know you from. Perhaps you've been a patient of mine?'

Bill, too, did a double take, but instead of concentrating his stare on Jack it was Anna who occupied his attention.

'It is, isn't it?' he said, breaking into a huge grin. He gripped Anna by the shoulders and hugged her to him. 'Anneka!' he said. 'Fancy meeting you again! I thought you'd moved out of the area.'

He stood back and looked at them both. The blood seemed to have drained from their faces.

'What is it?' He laughed nervously. 'What have I said? You both look as if I've done something awful.'

Anna was completely stunned—and speechless. *Who on earth was this man who seemed to know her? Or at least seemed to know Anneka?*

'Bill,' said Jack, his voice deep and calm, 'this is Anna. My wife, Anneka, died three years ago.'

Now it was Bill's turn to go chalk white. He stared at Anna and then at Jack and then back at Anna again.

'Oh, yes,' he said, his voice quavering. 'I can see that now. I can see that this isn't Anneka. My God, I'm so sorry, old man,' he said, grasping Jack by the shoulder. 'How awful for you.'

'What's going on?' asked Irene, as puzzled by the turn of events as Anna was. 'Bill, have you met Anna and Jack before?'

'I know Jack,' said Bill. 'He's married to...he *was* married to a Danish au pair who used to work for me five or six years ago.'

He turned to Jack. 'I got divorced a couple of years ago and then I remarried. The children live with my ex-wife.'

When they were on their own, Jack said to Anna,

'I'm sorry about that. Did it give you a nasty turn? It gave me one, I can assure you!'

Anna didn't respond at first but looked across the lawn in the vague direction of Bill and Irene.

'Anything the matter, Anna?' Jack asked. 'Did Bill's remark upset you?'

'No, he didn't *upset* me!' she snapped back, her happy party mood now evaporated. 'He annoyed me, that's all. The stupid man!'

'Don't let him upset you—'

'I've told you, I'm *not* upset! I'm annoyed with myself for letting him annoy me, and that's very annoying!'

Realising how foolish this sounded, she caught his eye and began to laugh. Jack slipped an arm round her and brushed his lips against her cheek.

'I love you when you're cross,' he said quietly in her ear. 'In fact, let's just say I love you.'

Anna's heart missed a beat. It was the first time Jack had told her that he loved her. She'd sensed it…the growing bond between them, the intense sexual attraction they had for each other…but until now the words 'I love you' had never been spoken. All thoughts of Bill and his clumsy remarks were banished from her mind. Jack had told her he loved her and nothing else mattered.

'I love you, too,' she whispered, her lips close to his.

The weather stayed fine—sunny and warm—and even when the food was served most people took their plates and found a space on one of the small lace-covered tables in the garden rather than using the chairs and long table in the mini-marquee. Which was just as well. The younger children, Saskia included, had decided to turn it into a den. They were having a fine old time, jumping on and off the folding chairs, playing hide-and-seek under the long tablecloth and racing round and round the table in a special game of 'tent tag' invented by the twins.

The food was delicious and Neil and Jennifer were almost as delighted with the compliments as Liz herself.

'I'm so relieved,' Jennifer confided to Anna. 'If it had been awful I'd have felt it was all my fault as I'd virtually insisted on us having Liz to cater. But she is good, isn't she? And her staff are superb...they really look the part in those white jackets and gloves.'

Anna agreed that the food was excellent. She even went back for a second helping of the vegetarian chilli.

When the main courses had been cleared from the mini-marquee, a large selection of mouth-watering desserts was spread out on the table. A large, beautifully decorated birthday cake was placed in the centre.

When the coffee was served, Liz carried the cake into the garden—sixty candles blazing away. Anna's father blew them out and everyone sang 'Happy Birthday'. The twins and Jasper were chosen to hand round slices of cake to everyone and they were very excited at being given this important role. The twins brought slices of cake to Jack's and Anna's table. They didn't leave immediately but stood shyly looking at each other and then at Jack and Anna.

They were whispering to each other, '*You* say it!', 'No, *you* ask them!' until Anna said, 'What is it you want to ask us?'

'We want to know if you're getting married,' they said in unison.

Anna blushed. *Children could be so direct and so embarrassing at times!*

But Jack was nonplussed. 'Why do you ask?' he said, smiling benevolently at the little imps.

'Because we want to be bridesmaids,' said one of them.

'Bridesmaids?' Jack laughed. 'Well, we'll have to see what we can do for you. You'll have to give us five minutes to think about it.'

'Right!' said the other twin. 'We'll be back in five minutes!' They both ran off, giggling.

'Sorry about that,' said Anna. 'Children can be so…'

'Children can be so right?' suggested Jack.

Anna shook her head. 'I was going to say so embarrassing.'

Jack reached out and took her hand. 'I'm not embarrassed. I'm delighted,' he said, his voice soft and velvety. 'You know I love you…and you said you loved me. I've been wanting to ask you to marry me—and now is the ideal opportunity. If you say yes, we can give the twins the good news about being bridesmaids.' His eyes were dancing with humour and she had no idea if he was serious or not.

'Are you seriously asking me to marry you?' she said, his sudden proposal taking her by surprise. 'Or are you playing a little game for the sake of the twins?'

His face darkened. 'I never play those kind of games, Anna,' he said. 'Proposing marriage isn't something I make a habit of doing…in fact, this is only my second time.'

CHAPTER FIVE

ANNA'S heart was moving so fast that she was breathless. So this was what it felt like when the man you loved asked you to marry him!

She'd imagined, somehow, it would be different—and certainly more private. In her imagination she'd pictured an intimate and romantic setting...just the two of them...and moonlight, maybe. Jack's proposal had been completely unexpected, triggered, it seemed, by two five-year-olds who wanted to be bridesmaids!

Looking across the lawn, she could see the two girls beginning to make their way back to her table. Jack noticed it, too.

'Here come the inquisitors!' he remarked. 'What's your answer, Anna? I really *do* mean it. I love you so much... I can't imagine life without you. Marry me...*please*.'

His eyes held hers and she was mesmerised by him. She'd never met anyone like him—and she couldn't think of anyone else she'd rather marry. Looking into his eyes she was convinced of his love...all the irritation and doubt she had felt when Bill had mistaken her for Anneka had vanished into thin air.

The twins had almost reached them as she said, 'Yes. I'll marry you.'

He leaned across the table and took her face in his hands, kissing her on the lips. As his warm breath touched her skin her body responded, sending her pulse hammering.

'They're kissing! They're kissing!' chorused the girls in excited anticipation.

'What's the answer?' piped up one of them when Jack and Anna finally pulled apart.

'The answer's "yes",' Jack announced triumphantly—much to Anna's consternation.

'Is that wise?' she muttered to him. 'I mean, the whole gathering is going to hear about it now. Just you wait and see!' Before she'd finished the sentence the twins were off, whooping and skipping with delight, shouting, 'We're going to be bridesmaids! We're going to be bridesmaids!'

Jack cupped her face and kissed her on the cheek, whispering, 'That's the whole idea. Now you can't change your mind!'

Anna felt hot blood flowing into her face and working its way through her whole body. Time stood still as realisation dawned. She'd agreed to marry Jack! It was the most important decision of her life and she'd made it hastily and with very little thought. She'd been aware for some time of her growing love for him—a love which had begun almost without her knowing it. She just hadn't expected him to move so quickly to a proposal of marriage! It wasn't in her character to act impulsively—and yet that was precisely what she'd done in saying 'yes' a few moments ago. Was this the end of the cool, calm Anna, the woman who hated being taken off-guard? She didn't know the answer to that, but she did know one thing...she'd never felt happier in her life!

As they'd predicted, the news spread as quickly as a bush fire. Within a very short time, Jennifer came hurrying across the lawn, accompanied by her two young daughters.

'Is this true, Anna?' probed Jennifer, eyes wide. 'Are you and Jack getting married? The girls said you promised they could be bridesmaids and I just wondered if they'd got the story wrong.'

Jack and Anna both grinned inanely at the anxious faces of Jennifer and the twins.

'It's all true,' said Jack, putting a proprietorial arm round Anna's shoulders. 'We're getting married. The sooner, the better.'

Jennifer's face was a picture. The tension lines vanished, to be replaced by a look of radiance.

'That is such good news!'

She kissed Jack and Anna. 'Can we tell everyone here today? It would make Dad's birthday even more special.'

'Go ahead,' said Anna. 'The twins will want to tell everyone they're going to be bridesmaids so we might as well get in first with the announcement.'

'I'll organise it,' said Jennifer, taking the twins by the hand and walking into the centre of the lawn. She clapped her hands to get everyone's attention.

'I've something wonderful to tell you,' she said. The twins were jumping up and down, unable to contain their hysteria. 'Jack and Anna have announced their engagement and they're going to be married very soon. Isn't that fabulous?'

One of the little girls tugged at her mother's sleeve. 'Tell them about *us*!'

'Oh, and most importantly, the twins are going to be bridesmaids.'

There was a murmur of approval and then a spontaneous burst of applause as all the family and guests clapped and cheered and toasted the happy couple.

Anna felt herself colouring up again.

'You look even more beautiful when you blush,' said Jack huskily. 'Who'd have thought that underneath that cool, sophisticated exterior beats the callow heart of a sixteen-year-old?'

They could see all eyes were on them so they rose and walked to the centre of the lawn to join Jennifer and the twins. Party guests crowded round them, offering congratulations. Anna's parents came over and hugged them both, saying how delighted they were.

'It's the best sixtieth birthday present you could have given me,' said her father with tears in his eyes.

Rebecca was equally thrilled.

'Now, listen, little sis,' she said, 'if you want any help in choosing your wedding dress then I'm just the person you need. And Ted with all his contacts in the clothing trade will be able to get you a really good discount.'

Anna kissed her on the cheek. 'Thanks, Rebecca. It's all happened so suddenly I just haven't had a chance to think about practical things like that. I'd be very glad of your help.'

The whole atmosphere of the party was raised to a higher level and everyone seemed to be smiling and happy. All, that was, except Bill Stone. Irene's new husband came over to Anna and, taking her by the elbow, moved her away from the main crowd. He had a very serious look on his face.

'Anna,' he said, 'I feel I must say something.'

'If you're going to offer to fly us to any honeymoon destination in the world free of charge, we'd be delighted to accept!' she quipped. But when she noticed that his face still stayed grimly serious the smile faded from her own. 'I was only joking, Bill. Is there anything the matter? You don't look too well?'

'I'm not feeling too good, that's for sure. But that's not what I wanted to speak to you about. It's about Anneka.'

The blood drained from her cheeks at the mention of Jack's first wife. Anneka was someone she had pushed to the back of her mind, particularly on the day she'd announced her engagement.

'What about Anneka?' she asked, fixing her face in a calm façade.

'As you know, she used to work for me as an au pair. She was with us for a fair amount of time—two or three years, I recall. My children were still at primary school.' His eyes went misty. 'They live with my ex-wife as she has custody, but I see them in the holidays.'

Anna folded her arms. Where was all this leading? Did Bill just want to relive old times? She smiled encouragingly.

'That's nice,' she said. 'And it must be good for Irene, too, because I don't think she had any children from her first marriage, did she?'

'That's right,' said Bill, rubbing a hand over his perspiring brow. 'About Anneka... She was a lovely girl...a bit of a handful at times, always wanting to stay out later than we said she should, that kind of thing. But she was very good with the children. And this is the point I'm trying to make, she looked *so* like you that you could have been twins.'

Anna breathed deeply. 'Yes, I do know that, Bill. I've seen her photograph—and you aren't the first person to make that comment. When Jack first met me he thought he was seeing a ghost.' She gave a hollow laugh. 'So don't feel you have to apologise for calling me the wrong name when we were introduced.'

'I'm not apologising,' said Bill. 'I'm warning you!'

'What?'

'I'm warning you not to marry Jack.'

'I'm sorry? What are you talking about?' said Anna, perplexed.

'He's doing it for the wrong reasons!' he said, his face turning puce as he spat out the words. 'It's obvious as the nose on my face. He only wants to marry you because you're the spitting image of Anneka!'

His vehemence took Anna off-guard and for a moment she was speechless. She stared at him, feeling as if she'd been punched in the stomach.

'I don't think you've any right to say that!' she said, after the shock of his words.

'I'm just offering you some friendly advice,' he said gruffly. 'Don't do it, Anna, because you'll live to regret it!'

She didn't know which of her conflicting emotions was the stronger—anger or distress. But as it turned out, she didn't have too much time to decide. The moment he'd finished speaking he put a hand out to steady himself and sat down heavily on a chair. Sweat was pouring off his face and he hugged his chest and stomach with his arms.

'Are you OK?' she asked with concern, wondering if he was having a heart attack.

Before he could answer he leaned forward and threw up violently, carefully avoiding getting any of the vomit on his designer suit.

'Oh, you poor man,' she said, putting a comforting hand on him. 'Have you been sick before? Are you being treated for any illness at the moment?'

He shook his head before throwing up again.

'Food poisoning,' he muttered between retches.

'You're sure you're not on any medication that might have had a bad reaction with the alcohol?'

'Look, lady,' he said, 'I'm a pilot. I fly all over the world, eat all kinds of food. I know food poisoning when I've got it!' He gagged again but by now his stomach was empty and nothing else spewed out.

'We'd better get you to hospital,' she said. 'I'll go into the house and see if anyone can drive you. I'll send Irene over to you.'

She delicately threw a napkin over the offending vomit and walked swiftly towards the house, telling Irene on the way to go and wait with Bill in case he collapsed. As she was about to walk into the house Neil came rushing out, looking as white as a sheet.

'I've just thrown up in the loo,' he said.

Rebecca came running towards her, waving her hands. 'Ted's not feeling well,' she said. 'He looks awful and I'm so worried about him. He looks as if he's going to faint and he has terrible stomach cramps!'

'Ask Jack to see to him,' she instructed. 'There are so many sick people that I'm going to have to call for an ambulance.'

By the time the ambulance arrived, eight people were needing to be taken to hospital—all of them, it turned out, having eaten the spicy beef curry. Ted, the worst affected, was stretchered into the vehicle by the paramedics.

'Did you have the beef curry?' Anna asked Jack as they were waiting for the back-up ambulance to arrive.

'I had the coronation chicken,' he said. 'It's Saskia's favourite. How about you?'

'The vegetarian chilli,' she said. 'Of course, it may not be the food that's the source of the trouble—it could be something they drank, maybe.'

'A bit unlikely, wouldn't you think? The beef curry seems to be the common denominator here. And the fact that the poisoning has worked so rapidly points to a staphylococcus toxin. That'd be my bet anyway. Most of the people affected seem to have strong constitutions,' he said, looking around the group clutching their stomachs and moaning intermittently, 'but I was a little worried about Ted. It's really not a good idea to get food poisoning when you're recovering from a major operation like he is.'

'I'll go and get samples of the food,' said Anna, 'and then we can have them analysed by the hospital path lab.'

Liz was very upset. 'I'm sure it can't have been my food,' she said when Anna asked for samples of everything. 'It's all prepared in the most hygienic manner. I'm an absolute stickler for keeping all my kitchen surfaces spotless. You could eat your dinner off my kitchen floor, I assure you!'

'It may not be the food,' said Anne. 'It might have been the champagne or some of the other drinks and I'm collecting samples of those as well. But we have to be sure about the food, if for no other reason than to rule it out.'

Jennifer was helping her put spoonfuls of food into separate polythene bags. 'Yes, Liz,' she said reassuringly, 'it's probably not the food at all.'

'Hope so,' said Liz.

'Don't worry, Liz,' said Jennifer brightly. 'Even if

it does turn out to be your food, it may not be too serious.'

Liz went puce. 'Of course it'll be serious! It'll be the end of me as a caterer! The end of *me*, full stop!'

She turned on Anna, eyes blazing. 'I'm in debt up to *here*.' She put her hand to the top of her head. 'This will sink me. I'll lose everything.' She grasped Anna's arm. 'If it is my food, can we hush it up? Can we keep it a secret?'

'Let's just see what the path lab comes up with,' said Anna. 'There's no point in worrying unnecessarily. And anyway, don't you think our first concern should be the people who've been taken ill? Jack was quite worried about Ted.'

'Oh, yes,' said Liz, pulling herself together. 'Yes, of course.'

When Anna had all the samples she drove to the hospital. But before she left she made sure that Saskia would be taken care of by her parents, Jack having gone on ahead with the 'walking wounded' in the second ambulance.

As she handed the samples to a lab assistant with instructions to test, as a priority, the spicy beef sample, her spirits took a dive.

What a fiasco! Their family celebration—the occasion of such happiness and joy—had turned into the party from hell. It wasn't just the food poisoning—with all its implications for those affected both healthwise and financially—but the truly upsetting episode when Bill had warned her in such brutal terms against marrying Jack.

It was only when the immediate emergency was over—all those affected taken to hospital and the samples delivered to the path lab—that she could slow down and consider what had taken place an hour or so previously.

She sat down on a chair in the corridor, not wanting to return yet to the A and E department where she knew Jack would be. She needed first to get her thoughts in some kind of order. Jack knew nothing about what Bill had said to her. Should she mention it? Or should she continue as if nothing had happened, hoping that their love for each other would be so evident that Bill's dire predictions would be of no significance?

Taking several deep breaths, she attempted to calm her nerves and concentrate her mind. She decided to take the latter course and not to tell Jack anything about her conversation with Anneka's former employer. After all, she loved Jack and he loved her, and that was all that mattered.

The following day Anna arrived early for her shift, keen to find out if there'd been any progress in identifying the cause of the sickness.

She'd heard that most of the guests had been allowed home after a few hours.

Until the bouts of sickness had subsided, they'd been given only water and told to take it in small sips. Once their stomachs had settled they were given larger quantities of liquid but told not to eat solid food for at least twenty-four hours but instead to keep on drinking lots of fluid.

The only patient who was still left in hospital was Ted. He had become dangerously dehydrated and was now in a special ward on an intravenous drip.

'How's Ted?' she asked Jack when she saw him in A and E.

'He's doing fine,' he replied, 'and your sister's with him at the moment.'

'Have the results come from the path lab?' she asked. 'At least then we'll know what we're dealing with.'

'They're getting in touch as soon as they've got a result,' replied Jack. At that instant his bleeper went. 'That'll probably be them now.'

He picked up the nearest phone. Anna stood next to him as he spoke to the lab.

'Thanks, Michelle,' he said to the lab assistant at the other end of the phone. 'You can check the other samples for anything else but I'm sure you're right with the spicy beef curry. We suspected as much.'

He replaced the receiver.

'Staphylococcus?' asked Anna.

Jack nodded. 'The beef curry was crawling with it. The lab manager wants details of the catering company because he's going to have to inform the health authorities. Do you want to put a call through to the caterers to make sure they've dumped all the contaminated food?'

'Yes, I'll do that,' said Anna. 'I don't know Liz's phone number but I'll call Jennifer—perhaps she's the best one to break the bad news. I feel desperately sorry for Liz...all her money's tied up in her catering business. I suppose they'll have to close her down after this?'

'Temporarily,' said Jack. 'But they really need to find the culprit...discover which one of her cooks has spoiled the broth, so to speak, by working with an infected cut or boil on his or her hands.'

* * *

Jennifer went almost hysterical when Anna phoned, giving her the news. She explained that the outbreak of food poisoning was probably due to one of the caterers—possibly Liz herself—having a skin infection. Bacteria would have been transferred to the food during preparation, growing and producing staphylococcus toxin. Once the food had been eaten the toxin would have rapidly produced symptoms.

'We need to contact Liz immediately,' she said, 'and the hospital laboratory will have to inform the health authority.'

'Poor Liz!' she wailed. 'Anna, can't you do something to hush it up—or at least stop the health people closing in on her? They're acting as if she's a criminal just because someone might have had a tiny boil on their finger! It's not as if she's done anything wrong! It was a genuine mistake, I'm sure...and anyway it was only a *little* mistake.'

'Jennifer,' said Anna, keeping her voice as calm and soothing as she could, 'your sister-in-law is responsible for the food she serves. She's a professional caterer. She knows the score. It's her responsibility to make sure that all her workers, and she herself, have scrupulously clean hands when they're touching food. If they've got any broken skin or infections on their hands, they should wear protective gloves.'

'You make it sound as if they're surgeons doing operations!' scoffed Jennifer.

'You make a good point. Surgeons wear latex gloves for a similar reason—to prevent cross-infection,' replied Anna, 'and if more caterers wore surgical gloves when they were preparing food, there'd be fewer cases of food poisoning, in my opinion. As far as hushing it up is concerned, Jennifer, you should know better than to ask. Ted is still on an intravenous drip as a result of Liz's "little mistake".'

Jennifer went very quiet at the other end of the phone.

'Liz must be told soon, if only to make sure that she's got rid of all the food from the party, particularly the beef curry. You can give me the number and I'll phone Liz if you don't want to do it,' suggested Anna kindly.

'No,' said Jennifer, 'I'll do it. I feel partly responsible anyway...we only had Liz doing the catering because I insisted.'

'In that case, you phone her but give me her details so that I can pass them on to the path lab.'

'Lunch?' said Jack when a quiet period happily coincided with Anna's rumbling tummy.

'Canteen?' she asked.

'Where else? I hear they've got a very tasty beef curry on the menu today.'

They strolled along the corridor that led to the staff restaurant.

'This is where we met,' said Jack. 'This exact spot.'

He indicated a square of vinyl flooring indistinguishable from all the others in the corridor.

'You're very precise,' she said, smiling.

He stopped walking and pointed into the distance, his eyes focusing on the canteen doors.

'I was standing here and you walked out of there,' he said, 'and my heart nearly stopped.' He reached for her hand and they carried on walking. 'And now you're going to marry me. I still can't believe my luck in meeting you like that.'

They reached the canteen doors and Jack slipped an arm round her, pulling her to him and kissing her.

'How do you fancy coming with me to Cornwall next weekend?' he asked when they were sitting down, eating their lunch.

'On holiday?' she asked. 'I'm afraid it's too short notice for me to get my rota changed.'

'Not on holiday,' he replied. 'Just there and back over the weekend. My parents live there and they're having Saskia for a couple of weeks. Christine wants to spend some time with her mother who's just had a hip replacement. It'll be a good opportunity to introduce you to your future in-laws.'

'That would be great,' said Anna enthusiastically. 'I'd love to meet them...and I haven't been to Cornwall for years, not since we had a summer holiday in St Ives when I was ten.'

'My parents live on the south coast of Cornwall, near Falmouth,' said Jack. 'They went to live there when Dad retired four years ago. They love having Saskia to stay...she's their only grandchild.'

'Have you told them we're getting married?' she asked.

'Not yet.' He covered her hand with his. 'I'm going to keep you as a special surprise.'

Anna had a far-away look in her eyes. She was trying to picture his parents, in a little house by the sea...and she was also thinking about Saskia's other grandparents. Whatever had happened to them?

'Penny for your thoughts?' said Jack.

'I was just wondering about Anneka's parents. Does Saskia ever see them?'

Jack's face clouded.

'No,' he said brusquely.

Anna waited for him to be more expansive. After a few moments' silence she said, 'Why not? Why don't you tell me about them? You know everything about my family—even down to my sister's sister-in-law, Liz the caterer.'

'Anneka's parents were divorced when she was a child and she lost touch with her father. Her mother still lives in Denmark.'

'You're not in touch with her?'

Jack stared into his glass of water. 'Not since the funeral,' he said flatly. 'She blames me for Anneka's death.'

'How ridiculous!' said Anna, frowning. 'How on earth could you be held responsible for a freak postnatal incident that was totally unexpected? You couldn't possibly have known that she was going to have a ruptured aneurysm!'

'No. But having a child, giving birth and everything which that entails may have exacerbated an existing, undiagnosed condition. Of course you're right in saying that it couldn't have been predicted, given that she didn't appear to have any symptoms beforehand. But if she hadn't had the baby she might have been alive today—that's always a possibility.'

'And Anneka's mother blamed you for that? What a callous woman!' Anna was still puzzled by the woman's strange response. 'Surely, when she'd got over the shock of her daughter's death, she'd have been more than keen to play a part in Saskia's life?'

'She wouldn't even look at the baby in the hospital,' said Jack bitterly. 'She knew that Anneka never wanted a child...strange really when you consider that her job had been looking after children. But she was adamant about it... And then she got pregnant

GET FREE BOOKS
and a
FREE GIFT WHEN YOU PLAY THE...

LAS VEGAS
GAME

▼ DETACH AND POST CARD TODAY! ▼

Just scratch off the gold box with a coin. Then check below to see the gifts you get!

YES!
I have scratched off the gold box. Please send me my **2 FREE BOOKS** and **gift for which I qualify.** I understand that I am under no obligation to purchase any books as explained on the back of this card. I am over 18 years of age.

M3AI

Mrs/Miss/Ms/Mr _____ Initials _____

BLOCK CAPITALS PLEASE

Surname _____

Address _____

_____

Postcode _____

7	7	7
🍒	🍒	🍒
🔔	🔔	☘

Worth **TWO FREE BOOKS** plus a **BONUS** Gift!

Worth **TWO FREE BOOKS**!

TRY AGAIN!

Visit us online at
www.millsandboon.co.uk

Offer valid in the U.K. only and is not available to current Reader Service subscribers to this series. Overseas and Eire please write for details. We reserve the right to refuse an application and applicants must be aged 18 years or over. Offer expires 30th August 2003. Terms and prices subject to change without notice. As a result of this application you may receive offers from Harlequin Mills & Boon and other carefully selected companies. If you do not wish to share in this opportunity, please write to the Data Manager at the address shown overleaf. Only one application per household.

Mills & Boon is a registered trademark owned by Harlequin Mills & Boon Limited.

The Reader Service™ — Here's how it works:

Accepting the free books places you under no obligation to buy anything. You may keep the books and gift and return the despatch note marked 'cancel'. If we do not hear from you, about a month later we'll send you 4 brand new books and invoice you just £2.55* each. That's the complete price - there is no extra charge for postage and packing. You may cancel at any time, otherwise every month we'll send you 4 more books, which you may either purchase or return to us - the choice is yours.

*Terms and prices subject to change without notice.

NO STAMP NEEDED!

THE READER SERVICE™
FREE BOOK OFFER
FREEPOST CN81
CROYDON
CR9 3WZ

If offer card is missing write to: The Reader Service, PO Box 236, Croydon, CR9 3RU

NO STAMP
NECESSARY
IF POSTED IN
THE U.K. OR N.I.

by accident...contraceptive failure. I persuaded her not to have an abortion. Anneka had discussed it with her mother on the phone nearly every day. She told her that she was only having the baby for me. Her mother even attempted to persuade me to agree to the abortion. So, when Anneka died so soon after giving birth, her mother blamed me entirely.'

'But Saskia? It doesn't make sense that she should take it out on the child.'

'She'd no time for the baby. "I've lost *my* daughter," she said, "so why should I be interested in *your* daughter?" That's why I consider that Saskia has only one set of grandparents. Talking of which, when we've dropped Saskia off I thought we could stop over for a night in the Cotswolds...in a wonderful country house hotel that I've heard about.'

'What a splendid idea,' agreed Anna.

'And then we can celebrate our engagement in true romantic style.'

He ran a finger under her chin and brushed his lips across hers. As he did so, all thoughts of Bill Stone and his woeful warning vanished completely from her mind.

CHAPTER SIX

THE drive to Cornwall took four hours. They stopped from time to time to stretch their legs—and once for a picnic lunch that Anna had prepared. It was the first 'real' picnic that Saskia had ever had and she was delighted with it.

'I want picnics *all* the time!' she declared, after realising that it didn't matter if you dropped crumbs or knocked things over because it was outside and Christine wouldn't be able to tell her off for being messy.

As they set off on the last leg of the journey, crossing into Cornwall, Anna was beginning to feel as excited as Saskia. There was something magical about the land and its natural beauty which she could sense even from behind the insulation of the car windows. Turning left off the main road, Jack drove them through the picturesque Cornish countryside which was dotted with the old workings of tin and copper mines, skirting quaint villages with ancient churches and historic inns, towards the small hamlet where his parents lived.

Their stone and slate cottage was at the end of a winding country lane. Jack parked the car outside and switched off the engine. He turned to Anna.

'We're here.'

'It's beautiful!' she exclaimed.

The front door opened and two people of a similar

age to her own parents walked down the garden path towards them. Anna clutched at Jack's arm nervously.

'They do know I'm coming, don't they?' she asked in a low voice so that Saskia wouldn't hear. 'You said you were keeping me as a surprise... I'm not sure that's such a good idea.'

'Relax,' said Jack. 'I told them I was bringing a girlfriend. I didn't tell them about the other thing—about us getting married. I wanted to tell them such momentous news in person, not over the phone.'

Saskia managed to unclip her own seat belt and was jumping up and down, impatient to be let out of the car.

'Grandma! Grandpa!' she squealed as Jack opened the door for her.

Jack greeted his parents who were very busy making a fuss of Saskia, telling her what a big girl she was and how much she'd grown since they last saw her.

After a few moments, Anna stepped out of the car and stood next to Jack. He put an arm round her and introduced her to his parents.

As she caught sight of her son's new girlfriend, Mrs Harvey's eyebrows shot up.

'Oh, you look like—' she blurted out, before she could stop herself. Jack's father intervened.

'You look like you could do with a nice cup of tea,' he said, smiling genially at Jack and Anna. 'And I hope you've come with big appetites because there's an enormous amount of food in there that your mother insists on referring to as "afternoon tea". More like the feeding of the five thousand,' he said with a grin, hoping that his wife's near-blunder had passed without notice. Jack's new girlfriend did look uncannily like his late daughter-in-law, but Mr Harvey, the embodiment of tact, would have been the last person to mention it.

'Come on, Saskia,' said Mrs Harvey, regaining her composure and taking her granddaughter by the hand, 'you can help me get out the cups and saucers for tea.'

'Anything you need carrying in?' asked Mr Harvey, peering into the car.

'A few of Saskia's things, Dad,' replied Jack. 'If you take the carrier bags full of toys, I'll bring in her suitcase.'

As they walked up the path, Mr Harvey said, 'You're not staying with us overnight, is that right? Your mother was in two minds about whether she should make up the spare beds.'

'We're stopping somewhere on the way back, a few miles from Stratford,' said Jack. 'Break the journey.'

Jack's father had been correct in his description of the extent of the afternoon tea. The table in the small dining room was covered with the most mouthwatering spread. Dainty sandwiches, home-made vol-au-vents and sausage rolls, a trifle, a chocolate cake and a large plate of scones which were piled high with strawberry jam and clotted cream.

'Since we retired to Cornwall my wife has gone native and become an expert on Cornish cream teas,' Mr Harvey told Anna. 'But we only indulge once a week—and when we have visitors. Otherwise my waistline would expand even more than it has already!'

Mrs Harvey was pouring out second cups of tea when Jack made his announcement.

'I have something to tell you all, and that includes you, Saskia,' he said, stroking his daughter's silky head. She looked up at him, her mouth surrounded by smears of chocolate and strawberry jam. 'Anna and I are getting married.'

'What's "married"?' asked the little girl.

'It means that Anna will come and live with us and be your new mummy. Would you like that?'

'I like Anna!' said Saskia, not really sure what all this was about.

'You can be a bridesmaid,' said Anna on a more practical note.

'Goody!' Saskia said, clapping her hands, before adding sweetly, 'What's a bridesmaid?'

They all laughed, releasing the tension of the moment. Judging by the initial shocked look on Mrs Harvey's face, Anna wasn't at all sure that it had been a good idea for Jack to spring the announcement on his parents. By the time she'd explained to Saskia about being a bridesmaid, Jack's mother was able to appear genuinely pleased about her son's impending marriage.

'I hope that you and Anneka will be very happy,' she said to Jack.

'Anna, Mum,' corrected Jack swiftly.

'Oh, yes,' said his mother, flushing a deep red. 'Anna, of course.'

They left soon after tea, Jack explaining to his parents that they had quite a few miles to drive to get to their hotel in the Cotswolds.

Saskia waved them off and then happily returned to playing a special game invented by her grandfather. It was called 'rabbits' and involved hiding behind the sofa and occasionally scurrying out to pick up imaginary carrots from the rug in front of the hearth.

Jack drove as fast as the speed limits would allow, keen to reach the Cotswold Hills as quickly as possible.

'I booked a room with a four-poster bed,' he said as they arrived at the country house hotel.

'I've never slept in one of those before,' said Anna, taking in the beautiful Tudor manor house with its mellow brickwork and golden Cotswold stone.

'I'm not planning on letting you get much sleep in this one either,' whispered Jack huskily in Anna's ear.

They checked in and were shown to their room, which not only had a four-poster bed but original oak beams and breathtaking views from the mullioned windows.

'Just think,' he said, as he joined her at the window looking out on the gently rolling countryside and parkland below, 'William Shakespeare was allegedly caught poaching deer in this park.'

'Would that be before or after he met Ann Hathaway?' said Anna. 'Before, I think, don't you? The love of a good woman often has a reforming effect on a man!'

'Is that what you think?' said Jack, squeezing her tightly in jest. 'Which reminds me...I've got something for you.'

Anna kissed him seductively. 'Let's have a shower first.'

'Shameless hussy,' he said, sliding his hand inside his jacket and pulling out a small box. A ring-sized box. 'This is for you...to make our engagement official.'

Anna opened the box and smiled with delight when

she saw the ring. It was a simple, solitaire diamond set in a band of gold.

'If you don't like it, or if it doesn't fit, we can change it,' said Jack anxiously.

'It's beautiful,' she said, taking it out and slipping it on her finger. It fitted perfectly. 'I'm going to wear it for ever,' she said. 'Even in the shower.'

An hour later, they made their way downstairs to the restaurant and were shown to their table. Anna glanced around the room admiringly.

'Looks a classy place,' she said, pleased that she'd thought to pack her 'best' dress in her overnight bag. The jade-coloured silk dress had a low, scooped neckline and elbow-length sleeves which rippled softly against her arms as she moved. The dress clung to her slender body, emphasising every curve from breast to thigh. Around her throat she'd clipped a simple chain made of thick links of 18-carat gold—a twenty-first birthday gift from her parents. It was the only jewellery she'd ever worn—up until tonight. Now, on the third finger of her left hand, sparkled the large solitaire diamond engagement ring.

Jack was studying the menu and the wine list.

'I've heard they've got a classy chef to match these surroundings,' he said. 'I'm glad we resisted eating too much of Mum's cream tea.'

Even so, for some reason neither of them was desperately hungry—not for food anyway. They each ordered a light main course of monkfish with a Caesar salad, followed by a warm plum and almond tart.

The chilled bottle of Chablis arrived and was placed by the wine waiter in an ice bucket. Raising their wineglasses to each other, they toasted their engagement.

'This is our celebration meal,' said Jack, his eyes meeting hers in the candlelight, 'but the real celebration comes later.'

A wild, sweet sensation swept through her and suddenly she realised why she had no appetite for food. Another hunger was shouting to be satisfied.

After the meal, having declined coffee—'We'll have no problem keeping awake,' growled Jack in her ear—they left the restaurant and made their way to their room. They held hands as they approached the door, fingers intertwined.

They went inside and closed the door, but not before hooking the 'Do Not Disturb' sign on the outside knob. He switched on one of the bedside lights which cast a soft glow over the four-poster bed and its luxuriant draperies. Their eyes held each other's and Anna felt her heart begin to beat fast.

As he removed his jacket and tie Anna felt a quiver of sexual excitement and anticipation. He moved to her and unzipped the back of her silk dress, slipping it down her shoulders and letting it drop to the floor. They took off their remaining clothes and stood naked in front of each other.

'You're so beautiful,' he said, taking her in his arms. At the touch of his body, lean and hard, she moaned. He lifted her up and carried her to the bed, lying down next to her.

He kissed her mouth with lips hot and burning, and ran exploring hands down her body. She sighed, eyes shut and weak with desire, yielding to the caressing movements of his fingers.

'I love you, Jack,' she said, clinging to him. 'I love you so much.'

'And I love you... From the first moment I saw you I wanted you.'

He covered her body with his own and they kissed hungrily, her body arching to receive him. She wound her arms round his neck as she went through wave after wave of piercing sweetness.

'Oh, Jack!' she called out involuntarily.

'Oh, Anneka, my love!' he cried in urgent response.

Afterwards she lay still, a shaft of ice piercing her heart.

Did he know what he'd said? In the half-light she looked at him. He had settled down under the bedclothes, his body relaxed and his eyes closed. One arm was languorously flung over towards her, his hand touching her as he drifted into sleep.

She, on the other hand, was wide awake and rigid.

She forced herself to face the possibility that Jack was not in love with *her*—but still in love with *Anneka*. Was she just a replacement for his dead wife? Everyone who'd known Anneka seemed to think so. Over and over in her mind she relived those moments when four people—Christine, Bill Stone, and Mr and Mrs Harvey—had first set eyes on her. She'd read it in their faces. *Jack's found someone just like Anneka*, they'd seemed to be saying to themselves. Only Bill had had the nerve, or the tactlessness, to say it to her face. And now she had all the confirmation she needed—from Jack himself! At the moment of love, at the height of his passion, whose name had he called out? Anneka's!

She moved out of his embrace, putting a distance between their two bodies. The action jolted Jack from his slumber and he reached out for her.

'Hey, don't leave me,' he said drowsily. 'Let's fall asleep in each other's arms.'

'Like you used to with Anneka?' Her face was against the pillow, muffling her bitter words.

He didn't hear what she'd said and, moving closer to her, he gently pulled her to him, positioning the curve of her back against his chest. He draped an arm over her hip and stomach, his hand drawing her towards him. She could feel desire rising in him again.

She moved away from him, her body tense and unresponsive.

'What's the matter, angel?' he asked sleepily. 'Have I worn you out? I'm just about to start wearing you out again.' He put his hand on her breast, his fingers searching teasingly for the nipple.

She pushed his hand away and sat bolt upright.

'It's not going to work, is it?' she said, choking back a sob.

Jack switched on the bedside light and turned to her, blinking. 'What are you talking about? What isn't going to work?'

'*Us!* You and me!' She buried her face in her hands and wept.

'Darling, darling,' he said his voice full of concern. 'Whatever's the matter? Was I too brutal, too forceful? It was just that I wanted you so much that I might have been—'

'No! It's not that!' She wiped her eyes with the back of her hands. 'It's not *me* you love, is it? I must have been blind not to realise it before. You're still in love with Anneka!'

Jack leaned on one elbow and stared at her.

'I love *you*. You must know that. And if you come back into my arms, I'll show you just how much!'

'I'm not talking about *making* love! I'm talking about being *in* love! Ask yourself, Jack, *who* you're in love with. Ask yourself honestly. I think you'll find it's still Anneka—or why else would you call out her name when you're making love to me?'

Jack's mouth dropped open. He was speechless.

'At least you have the honesty not to deny it!' she said.

'You must believe me, Anna, if I called out her name it was a mistake.'

'A mistake? This whole thing has been one big mistake!' She gazed up at him, a mist of tears filling her eyes. 'How can we be engaged, hoping to spend a lifetime together, when you're actually in love with someone else?'

She touched her ring, slowly turning it round her finger. The action sent a jolt of alarm through Jack.

'Let's not overreact here! You're not thinking of breaking off our engagement, are you?' he asked.

'Of course I am!' She stared down at the ring, pulling it off her finger decisively. She banged it down on the bedside table. 'You don't love me so there's no point in us being engaged.'

'You're being childish!' he said angrily, shocked by her action.

'How dare you call me childish?' she said, raising her voice in a way she'd never done before.

Anna couldn't believe how emotional she'd become. It was so unlike her, so out of character. But the emotional roller-coaster that she'd experienced in the past few hours had totally changed the way she would normally have reacted. At least with Liam she'd been able to keep some semblance of dignity...but now, having come this far with Jack, a man she loved desperately, only to discover that he too didn't really love her, was just too much to bear. She broke down and wept bitter tears.

Jack was appalled. He put his arms around her and held her closely to him.

He wanted to tell her that he loved her for herself, for her warmth and humanity, for the ways she made him laugh, for the way she made his heart stop every time he saw her. He wanted to tell her that making love to her had been one of the most wonderful moments of his life. But he knew that she wouldn't believe him…and all because in an unthinking moment he'd called out someone else's name.

He held her until she'd stopped crying. Then he touched her cheek, gently tracing the line of her chin down to the hollow of her neck. 'Believe me, the last thing I ever wanted to do was to hurt you. Please, don't break off our engagement. If you do, you'll break my heart.'

There was an anguished tone in his voice that sent a shiver of remorse through Anna. She propped herself up on one elbow.

'Well, I'm not sure…'

He could sense she was wavering and he took his opportunity. 'We can make it a trial engagement,' he suggested, almost pleadingly. 'People have trial marriages, so why not a trial engagement?'

'All right,' she said at last. 'We'll stay engaged, Jack, just as long as you realise that I'm not prepared to be a substitute.' Her voice was calm but firm. 'And I don't think it's a case of my overreacting or being childish. You must have been aware of the reaction of everyone who'd known Anneka…they all seem to believe you're trying to replace her with me. One of them actually warned me not to marry you!'

'That's a ridiculous suggestion!' protested Jack. 'And who's been going round warning you about marrying me?'

'Bill Stone.'

'I'll push his teeth down the back of his throat,' snarled Jack in anger. 'What the hell was the man thinking of? How dare he *warn* you about me?'

'I think he believed he was giving me a bit of friendly advice.'

'Huh!'

'But it's wasn't just Bill…it wasn't just you calling out Anneka's name…it's a combination of everything, even down to our first meeting when you thought you'd seen a ghost. Don't you see, Jack, our whole relationship is tainted by my resemblance to your first wife. I don't *want* to be a second Anneka! I want to be myself and not a replacement for the wife you lost.'

'I'm sorry,' he said softly, almost inaudibly. 'I'm sorry if I've hurt you, Anna. Believe me, it was unintentional. Believe me when I say I love you. The trouble is, I have no way of convincing you.' He looked at her pleadingly. 'Don't let that one word ruin a lifetime of happiness, Anna. Give me another chance to try and show you that it's you I love.'

She listened with lowered eyes to what he'd said. Perhaps she was being too harsh on a man who'd been through so much—perhaps she herself was being over-sensitive after her treatment by Liam, afraid to trust a man again. She flicked a look at Jack, now lying across the bed, his hair tousled, an agonised expression on his face. She loved the man, loved him so much it hurt. Surely she'd be mad to throw away so easily the chance of happiness? She must walk away from the shadow of Liam's betrayal and learn to trust Jack.

'I love you,' she said carefully, 'but I have to be sure you really want *me* as your wife, not a clone of Anneka.'

He sat up and put a finger over her mouth. 'Please,' he whispered, 'just forget it ever happened—for both our sakes.'

She picked up the ring and put it back on her finger. Jack breathed a sigh of relief.

Then he kissed her tenderly on her damp cheek and turned out the light. For a long time Anna remained awake unable to sleep. Was it possible for her to forget it had ever happened? However much Jack reassured her, somehow a light had gone out from the blaze of happiness she'd felt at their engagement.

CHAPTER SEVEN

'WHAT a pleasant surprise!' said Rebecca as she opened the front door and found her sister standing on the doorstep.

Anna smiled brightly. 'I was just wondering how Ted was now that he's back home again.' She followed Rebecca through the hall and into the living room.

'See for yourself,' said Rebecca, pointing to her husband who was sitting on the sofa, reading a magazine.

'Hello, Anna,' he said, about to stand up and greet her.

'Please, don't get up, Ted,' said Anna, 'and that's doctor's orders!' She kissed him on the cheek. 'How are you feeling?'

'Much better,' he replied. 'My insides feel as if I've had a good kicking from an angry donkey—and I've probably had my recovery from the spleen operation set back a couple of weeks—but, fingers crossed, everything's going to be fine from now on.'

'Glad to see you're not busy doing any work,' she said, pointing to the colour supplement magazine.

Ted grinned and showed her the page he'd been reading. It was a feature on ladies' underwear.

'Just checking up on what the opposition are doing this season,' he said. 'VPL is something I'm struggling with at the moment.'

'What?' said Anna, imagining some strange new illness Ted thought he'd contracted.

'Visible panty line,' supplied Rebecca. 'Ted's company believes that we girls are obsessed with it and talk of little else. The manufacturers are vying with each other to come up with the best solution—from which they'll make lots of money, no doubt.'

'Fascinating,' said Anna, who over the years had become used to Ted's strange business-related topics of conversation.

'Will you have a cup of tea?' asked Rebecca. 'I've just made a fresh pot.'

'That would be lovely.' Anna sat down next to Ted on the sofa. He closed his magazine and put it to one side.

'Don't let me stop you delving into the mysteries of VPL,' said Anna, trying to keep a straight face.

'I've read it. I'd much rather hear about the exciting goings on in your A and E department.'

Anna laughed. 'No, you wouldn't. And anyway, you've spent a fair bit of time in there yourself recently. I'd have thought that was plenty to last you a lifetime.'

'I was referring to you and Mr Harvey. How do you find it, working together, you and your fiancé? Is it like in those medical soaps on TV—lots of hanky-panky in the sluice room?'

Rebecca came breezing into the room with a tea-tray, having overheard her husband's last remark.

'Mind your own business,' she told him. 'That's girl-talk, and if you're not careful we'll take our tea into the kitchen and gossip away where you can't hear us!' She ruffled his hair playfully.

Anna took the china mug that her sister handed to

her. For some reason she found herself unable to make small talk, unable to chat in a natural way. She'd called round to Rebecca's just for a sisterly visit. But the moment Ted had started being jokey about her and Jack, her mind had gone blank. All her doubts about their engagement and forthcoming marriage seemed, once again, to well up inside her. She stared mutely into her cup before taking a couple of sips.

'Is there anything the matter, Anna?' Rebecca had given Ted a quick glance to see if he'd any clue as to why her sister was so quiet. Ted had shrugged.

'No, not really,' said Anna haltingly, unable to share her worries with her sister and brother-in-law.

There were times, and this was one of them, when she wished she wasn't such a private person. How she longed to open up and bare her soul in front of these two kind and caring people—but she just couldn't do it. She took another sip of tea. There were, however, two people that she *could* open up to, she realised—her parents. Her mother in particular would know exactly how she felt and be able to empathise with her. She had intended to see them later that day, but now she felt the urge to go round sooner.

'I won't stay too long. I want to call round on the Gypsies,' she said, draining her cup. 'We have to catch them while they're still here—I heard they were planning their next trip already!'

When Anna left Rebecca's she drove the short distance to her parents' apartment.

'Lovely to see you, darling,' said her mother, hugging her. 'Anna's here!' she called out to her husband.

'We know how busy you are at the hospital and how precious your spare time is.'

'I'm never too busy to see you both, you know that, Mum. I've come to hear all about your next trip.' She followed her mother into the living room where her father was sitting surrounded by maps and travel books.

They chatted for a while about the various merits of the individual countries that were under consideration.

'We're quite keen to go to Scandinavia this next trip,' said her father. 'We're torn between Denmark and Norway. Perhaps we'll do both—and we might even tackle Sweden and Finland at the same time. What do you think, Anna?'

'Yes, do them all,' said Anna, not really concentrating on her reply. At the mention of Denmark the image of Anneka flashed into her mind and she couldn't expel it. She became pensive, brooding on the larger-than-life poster of Jack's first wife that was hanging on Saskia's bedroom wall.

'Anything the matter, love?' asked her mother softly.

Anna shrugged, gulping back tears.

Her mother put a comforting arm around her. 'Come on, Anna, I know when something's troubling you. From when you were a little girl I could tell when you were keeping worries to yourself and trying to cope with them on your own. Is it Jack? Is there a problem between you two?'

Anna remained silent for a while, leaning against her mother. It was a long time since she'd let herself be treated like a small child and she found it a most soothing experience. After a while she pulled herself away.

'I'm not sure if there is a problem or not,' she said, 'but there is something troubling me about the relationship. The problem, if it is one, is that I happen to look very like Jack's first wife, Anneka. In fact, I'm her spitting image.'

'The poor woman who died in childbirth?' asked her mother.

'Shortly after giving birth, yes.'

'So why is that a problem?' asked her father.

She spread out her hands in a gesture of futility. 'It just *is*, that's all! You see, I'm not sure if he's marrying me for the right reasons. In fact, I'm convinced he's marrying me for the wrong reasons—and that he only wants me as a replacement for Anneka, his dead wife.'

Her father was the first to react, going red in the face and raising his fist in the air.

'If that man hurts you, in any way, he'll be sorry!' he stormed. 'A replacement for his dead wife! What a callous way to carry on!'

'Dad!' said Anna, alarmed that her father might go round straight away and confront Jack. 'It's only a feeling I have, that's all. Jack denies it. He says that I'm imagining it all…and he may be right.'

'Oh,' said her father, calming down.

'I don't think Jack set out deliberately to find someone who looks like Anneka—he admitted as much,' said Anna, 'but, looking the way I do, it's very hard—for both of us—to know if he really loves *me* or if it's just superficial and purely down to the way I look.'

'Then *change* the way you look,' said her mother in a practical tone of voice.

'What? Dye my hair black or dark brown?' Anna laughed at the notion.

'Why not?' replied her mother. 'Cut it short and curl it, if you want. Anything to make yourself look totally different from his late wife.'

Anna's father jumped up in protest. 'What sacrilege!' he said, staring at Anna's straight, blonde hair. 'Jennifer and Rebecca have inherited the dark brown hair from your side of the family,' he reminded his wife. 'The Italian connection.'

'In the very distant past!' interjected her mother.

'Anna's got the blood of the Vikings from my side of the family,' he stated.

'But you're from Yorkshire!' said Mrs Craven with mirth.

'Exactly!' responded her husband in triumph. 'And where do you suppose all those blond Scandinavian warriors ended up after they'd jumped off their longboats? Yorkshire, that's where!'

'Is that why you're so keen to go to Scandinavia—to look up a few relatives?' she asked, smiling at him warmly. 'I doubt if you'd find many after a thousand years!'

As her parents exchanged mock insults about each other's ancestors, Anna became thoughtful. Maybe her mother had a point. Maybe, just *maybe*, if she changed her appearance, she would find out if Jack's love was purely skin deep.

'Mmm,' she said, 'I think you might just have had a brilliant idea, Mum. I'll phone my hairdresser and fix an appointment straight away.'

'Now look what you've done!' Mr Craven said to

his wife. 'We won't recognise our daughter next time we see her!'

Anna kissed him on the cheek and gave him a hug. 'Yes you will. I'll wear a rose between my teeth and we can have a secret password.'

An hour later, Anna left their apartment, feeling a whole lot better than when she'd arrived. Her mother's idea had lifted her spirits, giving her something positive to do. Now she felt that by taking the initiative and changing her appearance she might discover the truth about Jack's love...was it real or fake?

'You want me to do what?' asked her hairdresser when she phoned for an appointment.

'I want my hair cut, curled and coloured dark brown, a really *dark* brown.'

There was an intake of breath at the other end of the phone. 'I *thought* you said that. I can fit you in tomorrow,' said Kieran, 'I've got a cancellation. But I'm going to get you to put this in writing! I don't want you suing me when you see all your golden locks on the salon floor and a mass of brown curls on top of your head.'

'I suggest we use a semi-permanent rather than a permanent dye,' said Kieran the following day as he snipped away at Anna's hair. 'Then, if you decide you've made a horrible mistake, it won't be so hard to remove. Now, I'll ask you for the third time, are you sure about this?'

'Believe me, Kieran,' she said, staring at her face in the mirror, 'I've never been surer of anything in my life. Well, perhaps that's a slight exaggeration.

But I'm determined to go ahead with it because I want a complete change of image.'

'Ah!' said the hairdresser knowingly. 'Boyfriend trouble.'

Anna pointed to her engagement ring. 'Not at all,' she said. 'I'm still engaged, if that's what you're wondering.'

She hoped Kieran hadn't noticed the way she'd blushed a little when she'd denied having boyfriend trouble. She certainly wasn't going to tell him the real reason for changing her image—to test whether or not Jack still loved her when she looked totally different.

'You surprise me,' he said sceptically. 'I can usually tell, you know. When a woman wants to change her hairstyle drastically it nearly always means the end of a relationship. They want a fresh start, unencumbered by the past.'

'Well, you're wrong this time, Kieran,' she said. But only by a whisker, she thought.

'If you say so. Now, about these curls. Loose or tight?'

'Somewhere in between.'

She leaned back in the chair and, closing her eyes, gave herself up to the agreeable experience of having her hair worked on.

The next day at the hospital was very amusing. Nobody recognised her—from the security guard to the nurse on the triage desk.

'You're going to need a new photograph for your security pass,' suggested the guard, who beamed at her when he eventually realised that this Dr Craven with the short, curly, dark brown hair was the same Dr Craven who used to be a long-haired blonde.

He stood back a pace to give her new look the once-over. 'Actually, it looks good. I've never been a great fan of blondes. I know they say gentlemen prefer them, but not me!' He gave a throaty chuckle. 'Perhaps that means I'm no gentleman!'

The reactions from the rest of her colleagues in A and E were mixed. Several raved about her new look, others were horrified.

'You must be barmy,' said one young nurse. 'I'd give anything to have long blonde hair like yours. Or, rather, like yours used to be!'

One female intern almost cried, her eyes brimming with tears when she saw what Anna had done.

'Don't worry,' said Anna comfortingly. 'It may not be for ever…the great thing about hair is that it grows!'

Anna didn't meet up with Jack until her lunch break. She walked over to his table with her tray. He looked up briefly as she approached and then went back to what he was reading. She could tell that in his first brief glimpse he hadn't immediately recognised her.

'Mind if I join you?' she asked in a low voice.

'Er, no,' he said. 'As long as you don't mind me carrying on reading this journal…'

He did a double-take.

'Anna?'

She smiled at him and he smiled back, laughing at himself for not realising who she was.

'Why are you wearing that wig?' he asked. 'Have you joined the hospital amateur dramatic society or something?'

'What do you think of it?' she asked.

He scrutinised her face and the short, dark curls that now surrounded it.

'It's not unattractive,' he said, giving an honest opinion. 'Quite sexy, in fact. But I think I prefer your real hair.'

'This is my real hair,' she said, her smile becoming more fixed and artificial.

'Come on, Anna!' He laughed. 'It's a wig!'

'No, it's not,' she said through gritted teeth. 'I decided to have a completely new look and decided on this.'

He stared at her in disbelief. 'You mean you've cut off your hair and dyed it black?'

'Dark brown,' she corrected. 'Black is a bit too harsh with my skin tone.'

'But why?' he asked in bewilderment. 'Why have you done it? And why didn't you discuss it with me first? I am, after all, your fiancé. Don't you think you might have consulted me before doing something as drastic as that?'

'It's *my* hair and I shall do exactly what I want with it,' she said defensively.

'I'm not being drawn into one of those kinds of arguments,' he said, an unbidden anger rising in his throat. 'I just want to know why the devil you found it necessary to change the way you look.'

'You seem to be putting quite a lot of store by looks. I hadn't realised it meant quite so much to you. I thought it was *me* you loved, not my long blonde hair that mirrored Anneka's!' She stared at him stonily.

He didn't react to her goading by flaring up—instead, he spoke very quietly, with a cold anger.

'I actually find that quite insulting,' he said, his

face going white. 'Insulting and offensive. Why are you still harping on about that one time when I mistakenly called out her name instead of yours?'

'I'm not,' she said. 'But I need to know if you still love me when I look different.'

'Then it's a matter of trust, isn't it?' He was still angry but his voice was now more reasoned. 'You should be able to trust me—just like I have to trust you. For all I know, I could be a dead ringer for this Liam fellow.'

Anna flinched as he said the name.

'We have to face reality,' said Jack. 'People often *are* attracted to the same kind of person. That doesn't mean they want a replacement, as you put it! I don't mind you cutting and dyeing your hair—shave it all off if you really want to—but do it because you want to and not because you're trying to test me.'

'Would you love me if I was bald?' she asked, trying to lighten the conversation. His impassioned reaction had taken her by surprise, but she was still glad she'd had the make-over...it would settle things one way or the other.

Jack dropped his head in his hands. 'Of course I'd still love you if you were bald. What is this? Some sort of mythological trial? Do I have to slay a dragon in order to win the fair maiden?' He sighed and looked up at her again. Then he saw the funny side of it and began to laugh.

Anna grinned at him, giving her head a little shake and letting the dark curls move slightly. 'You like it a little bit, don't you?' she asked.

He leaned back in his chair and took his time looking her over. He nodded slowly. 'It's not bad,' he admitted grudgingly. 'But promise me you won't rush off and have a make-over every time we have a disagreement about anything. Or at least give me a bit of warning if you're planning on becoming a redhead.'

She was glad the air had been cleared. She really hadn't intended her new image to upset Jack in the way it obviously had. His first reactions had been bad, but it was early days. Only time would tell, she decided, whether he now regarded her as a stranger and not the woman he thought he loved.

They finished their lunch and Anna left the canteen first, needing to get back quickly to A and E. As Jack watched her walk away his heart gave a lurch. It was obvious that she didn't trust him. Why else would she have bothered to make such a drastic change to her appearance?

He loved her...he knew that without the shadow of a doubt. Just watching the way her body moved, the distinctive sway of her hips as she walked, made him want to run after her and take her in his arms, dyed hair and all. But how could he convince her of his love? And how much was he to blame for making her feel so insecure that she'd needed to act in such a dramatic, over-the-top way? She was certainly right in her assumption that her likeness to Anneka had been the catalyst for their first meeting. And it had probably been the main reason he'd asked her out on that first date for a drink in the pub. But somewhere along the line, very early on, he'd stopped thinking of her in relation to Anneka because she was so totally different. And somewhere, a little further down the line, he realised that he'd finally stopped mourning his late wife and had been ready to move on. That had been when he'd realised that he loved Anna—

and that he would continue to love her whether she dyed her hair black, red, yellow or blue or all the colours of the rainbow! But trying to convince her of it could be difficult. Whatever he said was bound to be taken the wrong way!

He sighed and closed his journal. He didn't understand her—he didn't understand many women. Why were they so much more complicated than men? He couldn't concentrate on the article about trauma medicine any more—his mind was on other things, namely Anna Craven.

In the A and E department the red phone rang and one of the interns, Alex, answered it.

'Road traffic accident involving an ambulance,' he said. 'It was on its way here, carrying a patient with kidney failure. One of the paramedics and the driver are injured. They're sending another ambulance to transfer the kidney patient to hospital but we need to supply a flying squad to attend on site.'

Anna volunteered to go and so did Jack, who had just arrived in A and E after an hour in Theatre.

'How's the kidney failure patient?' Jack asked. 'Is he injured, too?'

'Apparently not, but he needs to be rushed here a.s.a.p.,' replied Alex.

He watched them as they walked briskly out of the department. 'Can I come, too?' he called after them, 'I took the call!'

'OK,' said Jack. 'It sounds as if we'll be needing someone to accompany the kidney patient and at least two others to deal with the injured on the spot.'

The three of them speedily put on the special green and yellow high-visibility overalls and jackets used by the medics when they were working outside the hospital. On their way out they picked up their emergency bags and quickly made their way to the waiting ambulance.

As they sped along, blue light flashing and siren blaring, Alex pointed to Anna's hair.

'What d'you think of this?' he asked Jack. 'She gave us all quite a turn this morning. I liked it much better before.'

Jack raised an eyebrow as he caught Anna's glance.

'She looks great to me,' he said. 'You shouldn't be so superficial, Alex,' he told the young doctor, giving Anna's hand a squeeze as he spoke. He kissed the top of her head. 'Blonde or brunette, it makes no difference to me.'

'You don't have to pretend,' she muttered under her breath. 'I know you hate it.'

From inside the vehicle the three medics found it difficult to work out the exact route taken by the driver. All they knew was that he was going like a bat out of hell.

When they reached their destination they found a few onlookers staring at the scene of the accident where the ambulance had left the road, mounted the pavement and crashed into a metal lamppost which, mercifully, was still remaining upright—as was the ambulance. Thick strips of rubber had been left on the road surface from the vehicle's tyres.

A paramedic whom Anna recognised from the hospital came over to them. Blood was pouring from a cut on his head.

'What's the situation, Nigel?' Anna asked him. 'And are you badly hurt yourself?'

'No, just a small cut. I was lucky,' he said. 'We

need to get our patient to hospital straight away—he's got kidney failure.'

'He'll be going in the ambulance we came in,' said Jack to Nigel. 'Alex and you can go with him. And get that cut looked at when you've delivered the patient. How are the others?'

'The driver is trapped but not injured too badly as far as I could ascertain.'

'What's his name?'

'Dave. And Ruth, the other paramedic, got thrown around during the impact and banged her head. She lost consciousness for a short time.'

The wailing sound of a siren heralded the arrival of a fire-engine. Working in tandem, the medical team and the firemen began to sort out the mess that had resulted from the crash.

The kidney patient was stretchered into the ambulance which then returned to the hospital, the patient being accompanied by Nigel and Alex.

'You take that one,' said Jack to Anna, indicating the female paramedic sitting at the roadside, 'and I'll take the driver.'

'Are you in much pain?' Jack asked Dave.

'Nothing I can't cope with,' he replied, 'but my neck's at a funny angle.'

Jack began to examine him as best he could, given the limitations of the crushed cab. 'Can you remember what happened to cause the accident?' he asked.

'I think there must have been a patch of oil on the road because I suddenly went into a massive skid. The ambulance spun out of control and ended up like this.'

A fireman standing next to Jack confirmed Dave's suspicions.

'There's an oily patch twenty-five metres back,' he

said. 'We're going to use the oxyacetylene torch to cut you free, mate, but there's quite a bit of petrol spilled onto the road so first of all we're going to have to put some foam on the surface to keep the fumes down.'

'Be careful when you release him,' Jack told the fire officer. 'I suspect he's got neck injuries. I'll put a firm collar round his neck to immobilise it now.'

Jack got the neck brace from his emergency bag and fitted it carefully round Dave's neck.

'That should immobilise it for now. Just relax and try to keep that neck as still as you can. If your pain gets worse, just ask me for a shot of pethidine. I'll be back in a moment. I'm just going to check on your colleague.'

Anna was with the injured paramedic, Ruth.

'Any problems here?' Jack asked.

'Ruth has a headache and slightly blurred vision,' replied Anna. 'I've checked her eyes and the pupils are reacting well. She has a small wound on her scalp, which doesn't appear to be serious. I've looked in her ears and I think there may be some blood behind the eardrums.'

'Fractured skull?' suggested Jack.

'A distinct possibility. Ruth was thrown quite violently against the inside of the ambulance.'

'I just missed catching my head on the corner of the metal first-aid box,' said Ruth. 'I'd have been knocked out completely if I had.' She put her head in her hands.

'Is the headache bad?' asked Jack.

'It comes and goes, like the blurred vision,' replied Ruth.

'There's another ambulance on the way,' he said.

'We'll get you back to the hospital for a CT scan and X-ray to check if you've fractured your skull.'

'I hope I've not got a brain bleed,' said Ruth.

'Even if you've got a skull fracture, the brain may not be damaged,' said Anna reassuringly. 'But the blow may have shaken the brain and bruised the tissue. You were unconscious for a short while, weren't you?'

'That's what Nigel told me. He cut his head and was bleeding a lot. Is he all right?' Ruth looked up at Anna and Jack.

'Nigel assured us it was just a surface wound. They'll give him a proper check back at the hospital,' said Jack, just as the wailing sound of another siren was heard. 'The ambulance is here. Will you be going back with Ruth?' he asked Anna.

'If you can spare me. Are you OK with the driver?'

'Yes. He's being cut out of the cab now and then I'll check him over. He seems to have got away with just a neck injury. Of course, until we X-ray him we won't know how serious it is. I've put an immobilising neck brace on him. You go back with Ruth and get her to the scanner as quickly as possible—that's a priority.'

Back at the hospital the news was good. The kidney patient was responding well to dialysis, and Nigel had had three stitches put in his cut and no further injuries were found.

Jack and Anna arrived with Ruth and Dave, who'd been released from the prison of his ambulance cab by the expertise of the fire crew.

Ruth was taken straight away for a brain scan and an X-ray of her skull. Dave's trolley was wheeled into

A and E for an X-ray using the portable overhead equipment. As they waited for the film to be developed, they checked his responses to stimuli to see whether his spinal cord had been damaged.

'Can you feel this?' asked Jack, touching Dave's left foot.

'Yes,' replied Dave.

Jack touched his right foot. 'And this?'

'Yes.'

He repeated the procedure with Jack's hands and forearms and received the same positive response.

'Any numbness or tingling in your hands?'

'No.'

Jack looked at Anna.

'So far so good,' she said. 'There doesn't appear to be any spinal injury.'

Jack checked Dave's eyes with a flashlight. 'No problem there either.'

The X-ray film arrived and Jack held it up against the light box. The two doctors studied it closely for signs of fracture or dislocation.

Jack pointed to one of the vertebrae. 'Slight damage here.'

He turned to Dave. 'It looks as if you've been very lucky,' he said. 'I'll give you a soft neck support to wear for the next few days, or weeks, until things settle down. I'll also give you a prescription for some strong painkillers. Don't go back to work until you can manage without the neck support.'

'What about some physio?' suggested Anna.

'Good idea. I'll arrange for twice-weekly sessions with the physiotherapist...and you can choose whether to come back here for check-ups or to go to your own GP.'

Jack and Anna went to find out about Ruth's results.

The X-ray had revealed a closed fracture of the skull—the kind of fracture that usually healed by itself. The brain scan showed a small amount of bruising.

'We'll keep our eye on that,' the neurologist told them. 'If there's any haemorrhaging, we'll do a craniotomy to drain the blood and repair any damaged vessels. But that doesn't look likely at the moment.'

'Will you be keeping her in the neurological ward for observation?' Jack asked him.

'Most certainly, particularly as there was some loss of consciousness.'

Jack and Anna walked back towards A and E.

'I must get changed out of these things,' said Anna, referring to her green and yellow overalls.

'Me, too,' said Jack. 'But first, how about five minutes for a coffee?'

'Make that four,' said Anna. 'I'm still on shift for another couple of hours.' She sighed wearily. 'It's been a long day.'

She smiled at him as they made their way to the canteen. 'Silly thing to say, really. They're always long days in A and E!'

'What are you doing tonight?' he asked.

'Having a lazy night in front of the TV.'

'Sounds perfect. Your place or mine?'

She pondered for a moment. 'Mine,' she said. 'I'm cooking Thai food for two at eight o'clock.'

He slipped an arm around her shoulder.

'You certainly know the way to a man's heart, Dr Craven.'

* * *

The Thai food was a great success if the empty dishes and Jack's satisfied look were anything to go by.

'That made a change from my frozen meals for one, I can tell you!' He drew her down on the sofa next to him. 'I guess I shouldn't have said that.' He nuzzled his face into her neck.

'Why not?'

'You'll be accusing me of wanting to marry you for your cooking!'

He ran his fingers through her dark curls and started kissing her.

Half an hour later, in the dishevelled comfort of her bed, Anna snuggled up to him. 'I thought we were going to watch TV,' she said.

'It's very thoughtless of you not to have a television in the bedroom,' Jack replied. 'I've got one in mine.'

'Is that an invitation?' she asked huskily.

'Invitation? You need an invitation?'

He took her left hand in his and felt for the engagement ring. 'That's your invitation,' he said. He ruffled her hair playfully. 'Even though I gave the original invitation to Goldilocks.'

She couldn't tell whether he was still annoyed with her for changing her looks. She was so happy at that precise moment that she wasn't even going to think about it, especially when he pulled her to him again, kissing her with a mounting fervour that was irresistible.

Three weeks went by. Saskia returned home from Cornwall and Christine moved back into Jack's house now that her mother was becoming more mobile after her hip replacement.

Jack suggested that he, Anna and Saskia go on a bike ride into the country.

'I've got a special seat on the back of my bike for Saskia,' he said. 'I often take her cycling at weekends.'

'I haven't got a bike,' said Anna.

'Can you borrow one?' asked Jack. 'What about your sisters?'

'Rebecca has one,' Anna remembered. 'She and Ted were on a health kick and they bought state-of-the-art machines for the whole family. I have a feeling that Rebecca's is still in pristine condition! I'll ask if I can borrow it...I'm sure she won't mind.'

'By the way,' asked Jack, 'what do your family think of the new look?'

He hadn't mentioned her change of image since the Goldilocks remark. She could tell by the surreptitious glances he kept giving her that he wasn't entirely happy about it, but he hadn't actually mentioned it until now.

'They like it,' she replied. 'My sister, Jennifer, says it makes me look like them. I think she has ambitions for us to form a singing group—the Craven Sisters, kind of thing.'

'It's an idea, I suppose,' remarked Jack. 'There might be more money in it than medicine.'

The cycle ride was arranged for the following Sunday. Anna borrowed Rebecca's bike and went for a spin round the block to get herself used to it. She hadn't been cycling since her student days when she'd owned an ancient sit-up-and-beg model with a wicker basket in front. Rebecca's bike had drop handlebars and a racing saddle.

'It makes your bum a bit sore if you ride for too long,' her sister confided as she handed over the gleaming machine.

'And how many times have you been out on it?' Anna asked.

Rebecca looked into the distance and, using her fingers to count, appeared to be doing a calculation. She then looked at Anna with an innocent expression.

'Once,' she said.

Jack cycled over to her apartment with Saskia seated at the back, wearing a tiny crash helmet.

Anna came out, also wearing a cycle helmet.

'Were you thinking that Saskia might not recognise you as a brunette?' Jack asked as she joined them.

'What's a brunette?' said Saskia, whose sharp little ears picked up everything.

'It's what I told you about, darling,' said Jack. 'Anna has a new hairstyle, a different colour. All the blonde hair has gone and now it's brown.'

'You needn't have made such a big thing of it,' she hissed under her breath. 'I was going to do it my way with Saskia, gently and slowly.'

'There's no gentle or slow way to do it,' he said close to her ear. 'The moment you took off that helmet the child would have got the fright of her life if I hadn't forewarned her!'

'You really hate it, don't you?' she said in a harsh whisper.

'Why are you both cross?' asked Saskia.

'We're not, darling,' said Jack. 'We're not, are we, Anna?'

He beamed at her, willing her to beam back, which she did.

'Of course not.' She kissed Jack on the cheek and

then kissed Saskia. 'I'm *so* looking forward to our ride.'

'Me, too!' said Saskia

'Me, too!' said Jack.

They set off, Anna following closely behind Jack and Saskia until they reached a country road on the outskirts of the town. The traffic was much less and Jack and Anna rode side by side.

'Saskia likes going past this field,' said Jack, 'because of the ponies. We usually stop and stand by the five-bar gate and they come up to us.'

They dismounted and walked up to the gate. Sure enough, the three horses that had been grazing in the field moved towards them. Saskia squealed with delight as one of them put his nose over the gate, inviting a stroke.

'Have you brought any sugar lumps?' asked Anna.

'Daddy won't let me,' said Saskia.

'I'm not too keen on her holding out her tiny hand in front of such a large mouth,' said Jack. 'When she's bigger we will. I've promised her riding lessons as well. There's a riding school nearby and we've already been to speak to them.'

Anna smiled as he spoke so lovingly about his daughter and the plans he was making for her. He was the kind of father any small child would love…totally caring and generous. And sensitive, she admitted. Perhaps he'd been right about warning Saskia about the change of hair colour. After all, he knew his daughter better than anyone, so who was she to criticise him for it? She unclipped her helmet and, taking it off, revealed the dark curly hair underneath.

'Look, Saskia,' she said, 'I've had my hair made a different colour.'

The child stared at her solemnly. 'Daddy told me,' she said, after she'd satisfied herself that it really was the same Anna that she'd known before.

'And what did Daddy tell you?' Anna asked, knowing that she probably shouldn't have done, knowing that she was prying into the private world of Jack and his daughter. But, hell, she thought, she was going to marry the man and be a mother to his child. Didn't she have a right to know what he was saying about her?

But the moment Saskia answered, Anna regretted asking.

'He said that you didn't look like my mummy any more,' said the little girl with childish honesty.

Jack looked embarrassed. 'We were looking at the picture in Saskia's room at the time...that's what she means.'

CHAPTER EIGHT

'I'M GLAD you came round,' said Rebecca when Anna returned the bicycle. 'We were just talking about you.'

'Oh?' said Anna guardedly. What was Rebecca plotting now?

'Jennifer and I were just wondering if you'd set a date for the wedding. Come in and join us for a coffee and a gossip.'

Anna followed her sister into the kitchen and greeted Jennifer who was already getting an extra mug down from the shelf for her.

'So when's it going to be?' Jennifer asked. 'We've been debating the various pros and cons of weddings at various times of the year.'

Anna's heart sank. She really wasn't in the mood for this kind of conversation.

'We haven't decided yet,' she said.

'You'll have to get a move on, you know,' said Rebecca. 'Everything gets booked up months in advance. But first things first. Were you thinking of a winter, spring, summer or autumn wedding?''

'To be perfectly honest, it's something I haven't given much thought to.'

'We think you should,' said Jennifer, 'if only to fit in with the Gypsies' travel plans.'

'Yes,' conceded Anna. 'That's something else I haven't given much thought to.'

'You *do* want Dad to give you away, don't you?'

said Jennifer, eyes wide at the very idea of Anna walking down the aisle on her own.

'Don't be silly, Jennifer. Of course I want Dad to give me away.'

'Especially as he'll be paying for it!' said Rebecca.

Jennifer opened her diary. 'You could have a Christmas wedding,' she said. 'They're always home for Christmas. Or a spring wedding when they're back from their skiing trips. Summer could be a bit tricky because they go off for months at a time.'

'I'm sure the Gypsies will fit their holidays around Anna and Jack's wedding and not the other way round! Honestly, Jennifer, sometimes you can be very silly.' Rebecca looked at Anna and raised her eyes to the ceiling.

Anna shifted uneasily in her chair. This whole conversation was making her feel very tense. The wedding date was not an item she wished to discuss with anyone at this stage, she decided, not even with Jack.

'I'm unsure about things, that's all,' she said, choosing her words carefully.

'Unsure about what?' probed Rebecca. 'Unsure about Jack?'

'Partly...and partly about myself.' Anna shrugged her shoulders. 'Getting married is a big step—you two must know that. It certainly isn't something to be rushed.'

'Oh,' said Jennifer.

'Oh,' said Rebecca.

The three sisters sat in silence, contemplating their coffee-mugs.

'I think long engagements are deadly,' said Jennifer after a long pause.

'So tell me about Liz,' said Anna, deliberately

changing the subject. 'How is she managing after the food-poisoning episode?'

'She's doing fine, actually,' said Jennifer. 'In fact, I haven't seen her looking so happy in months. She's got a new man in her life!'

'Oh, I am pleased,' said Anna. 'I was actually meaning her business and whether that's picked up again after her short closure.'

'The two things aren't unconnected,' said Jennifer. 'The new man is the food inspector who came along and closed her down! The two of them hit it off immediately, she told me. Instant attraction. And, once the all-clear was given for her business, he was able to advise her on all aspects of food safety and that kind of thing.'

'I'm so pleased,' Anna reiterated.

'So, if you ever get round to choosing a wedding date, you might want to hire Liz for the catering!'

Both Anna and Rebecca turned to Jennifer and shook their heads.

'I'm sure she's great,' said Anna, 'but I still have this awful picture in my mind of all those people getting ill at Dad's party.'

'And I don't think I could persuade Ted to eat a mouthful of her food again—not after what happened to him last time,' said Rebecca ruefully.

'So where will you have the wedding reception when you and Jack finally decide to get married?' asked Jennifer, looking slightly miffed.

Good heavens! thought Anna. Whatever subject I bring up, Jennifer always manages to turn it round to the wedding plans—or lack of them! She put her hands up in mock surrender.

'I don't know,' she said. 'I don't care.'

'Leave the poor girl alone, Jennifer,' Rebecca chided. 'I'm sure she'll tell us all in good time.'

That evening Anna and Jack went to the local multiplex cinema to a film they'd both been wanting to see. There happened to be a wedding scene in it. Jack slipped his arm round her shoulders and whispered in her ear, 'That reminds me—we've got a date to fix.'

With a great effort she kept her voice calm and level as she replied, 'Yes'.

They called in at a pub on the way home for a quick drink. It was the one he'd taken her to on their first date and they now regarded it as 'their' pub. He bought a beer for himself and a glass of white wine for Anna.

'So,' he said as they sat close together at a corner table, 'about our wedding date. Any ideas when it should be?'

'Not really,' she said.

'I don't know about you but, speaking personally, it can't be too soon. I'd marry you tomorrow if it could be arranged.' He brushed his lips across her cheek.

'There are a lot of things to organise,' she said.

'Then the sooner we start the better.' He looked at her searchingly. 'What month shall it be? Next month? The month after?'

She was taken aback. 'Not so soon, surely? I thought you were happy with our trial engagement.'

As she spoke those words, the image of that evening in the Cotswolds flashed before his eyes. It was a painful memory and he felt himself flinch.

'I said a *trial* engagement, not a *long* engagement, if you remember.'

'Some trials can go on for a long time, though, can't they?' she said lightly.

'I'm serious, Anna. I think we should fix a date soon. We love each other and it's natural that we should want to spend every possible moment together...in the same house...in the same bed.'

'I could move in with you,' she suggested. 'Then there won't be quite the hurry to—'

'To get married?' Jack's facial muscles contracted as he said the words. 'Do I take it you're not in a hurry to get married?'

'Well, seeing you put it that way, no. I like things as they are. I like being engaged.' She looked at her ring as it sparkled in the artificial light.

'Piffle,' said Jack. 'Being engaged is neither one thing nor the other. And when I bring you to my house I want it to be as my bride. I'm an old-fashioned guy. I want to carry you over the threshold and all that kind of soppy stuff. I want to be able to say to people "This is my wife", not "This is my live-in girlfriend". And I also want Saskia to know where she stands with you. I'm not the kind of father who invites a succession of girlfriends to pretend to play house with me.'

Anna stared silently into her wineglass.

Jack gave a hollow laugh. 'I thought it was men who were supposed to be noncommittal where marriage was concerned! I hadn't realised I was getting myself involved with a woman with a marriage phobia!'

'I'm not against marriage...I just don't want us to rush into it.' She felt very miserable.

'I know what this is all about! It all boils down to

whether or not you trust me, doesn't it? And you know something, Anna? I don't think you do.'

'That's not true!' she protested.

'It all started because you thought I only wanted you as a replacement for Anneka. You said as much. And all this changing your hairstyle...and now not wanting to fix a date...it's all tied up with your obsession with my first wife.'

'It's not an obsession!' she said, keeping her voice low so as not to draw attention to the two of them. 'Can we talk about this somewhere more private?'

They finished their drinks in silence and walked out to Jack's car. He didn't start the engine.

'Where were we?' he asked. 'As I recall, we were at the point where you said "I don't really want to marry you."'

'I didn't say that!'

'In as many words, you did. Even when I say I like your hair you don't seem convinced.'

'That's because I don't think you do like it. You still prefer me as a blonde, don't you?'

'Yes,' he said, unrepentant. 'But what gets me about it is that if we were just a normal boyfriend and girlfriend, and you had a new hair colour and I said I didn't like it as much, well, you'd think, Oh, he doesn't like it as much. But instead, you think, Oh, he wants me to look like Anneka. I just can't win, can I? Yes, I prefer how you looked before. Is that a crime? It certainly doesn't mean I love you any less than I did before.'

'I'm sorry, Jack, but the doubts are there. I can't help it if they are.'

His hands were gripping the steering-wheel as he

stared out into the blackness. 'In that case, it's just as well we found out now, isn't it?'

'What do you mean?' she asked, a cold fear encompassing her heart.

'I mean that it's just as well we found out that you don't trust me. Just as well we found out before we got any further with this charade of an engagement. You know what "engagement" means, I presume? It means being engaged to be married! If there's no likelihood of that event taking place in the next twenty years, I suggest we call it a day.'

'End our engagement?' she asked, knowing what his answer would be.

'I'm not prepared to invest any more time or emotion in a relationship that has no future. If you don't trust me, that's all there is to it,' he said.

Anna stared ahead, her mind ablaze with conflicting emotions.

'Very well,' she said into the stony silence, and, twisting the ring off her finger, she placed it on top of the dashboard.

Jack ignored it and started up the engine. 'This has turned out to be one of the unhappiest days of my life,' he said.

His words echoed Anna's inner thoughts and she couldn't wait to get home and close her front door before opening the floodgates. Why couldn't she have told Jack that she trusted him? Was it because she didn't—and why did she still have doubts? Who was to blame for her insecurity? she mused on the journey home. She knew the answer well enough. Liam. The way he had trampled on her love had made her so distrustful of almost anyone else—including the man she loved more than anyone. Jack.

* * *

'Oh, no!' said Rebecca, coming over to the sofa and squeezing herself into the tiny space that was available, pinning Anna between herself and Ted. 'Jack and you have split up? That's terrible.' They each put an arm round her.

Anna had forced herself to come round to Rebecca's in order to tell her in person about the break-up.

'I'm very sorry,' said Ted.

'What a rat that Jack is!' said Rebecca. 'And he seemed such a nice, caring man and a really good doctor, too.'

'He's all those things,' said Anna. 'But it didn't work out. Let's just say we were incompatible.'

Ted gave her a squeeze. 'That old sex problem!' he said.

'Ted!' exclaimed Rebecca, embarrassed by her husband's remark. 'Honestly, Anna, that's all men ever think about!'

'It wasn't anything to do with that,' said Anna, heating up under her skin.

'No, of course it wasn't! That was a silly thing to say, Ted.' She glared at him over Anna's head.

But even as Anna denied that their break-up was connected with a sexual problem she found herself recalling vividly how, at the climax of his lovemaking, Jack had called out Anneka's name. That, she decided, wasn't something she would ever tell another soul—and certainly not her sister and brother-in-law.

'It just didn't work out the way we hoped it would,' she said. 'Therefore we thought it best to end the engagement.'

This time it was Rebecca who squeezed her. 'Yes, darling. We don't want you marrying anybody who isn't going to make you happy.'

The doorbell rang and Rebecca jumped up. Anna breathed out, relieved not to be trapped in the middle. She stood up just in case Rebecca returned and took up where she'd left off.

'If you're expecting someone, I'll leave,' said Anna. 'After all, I did call round out of the blue.'

Rebecca called from the hall, 'Stay, Anna. We're not expecting anyone.'

Anna heard her open the door and then exclaim, 'Well, hello, Jennifer. Do come in. You'll never guess who's also here!'

Rebecca and Jennifer came into the living room and Ted got up.

'I can see this is going to turn into a girlie meeting, so I'll leave you to it,' he said. 'I've got a brand-new computer golf game I want to try out.' He kissed Anna on the cheek and said, 'Chin up!' Then he greeted Jennifer with a similar kiss but without the words and left the room, closing the door behind him.

'Hi, Anna!' said Jennifer. 'How's that gorgeous fiancé of yours?'

Rebecca elbowed her in the ribs. 'It's off!' she whispered hoarsely.

Jennifer looked uneasy. 'Oh, no!' she said. 'You mean you're not getting married?'

'Got it in one, Jennifer,' said Anna. Then, realising she must have sounded a bit sharp, apologised. 'Sorry, I didn't mean to snap at you.'

Anna moved to a chair, deciding she didn't want to be squashed between her two sisters on the sofa and preferring the independence of her own space. 'I was just telling Rebecca and Ted that Jack and I are no longer engaged. We broke it off last night.'

'But you still work together, don't you?' said Jennifer, appalled at the news. 'Won't it be *awful* when you keep bumping into each other all the time? I once had a boyfriend that I worked with...I think I may have told you at the time. Anyway, when we broke up it was just awful seeing him in the office and I asked Personnel for a transfer to another department.'

Anna was quite happy to let Jennifer waffle on. Being as self-obsessed as Jennifer had its good points. It meant that you only had to introduce a topic and she would reel off yards of experiences that always involved herself as the central character. As she regaled them with reminiscences of how she had coped with this particular situation—'This boy and I weren't engaged, but *nearly* engaged...so I know what you're going through'—Anna drank the rest of her tea and found Jennifer's long-winded story surprisingly soothing.

Rebecca, however, was impatient to hear Anna's own story.

'Jennifer, all that happened a long time ago. We need to help Anna at the present time.'

'That's what I'm trying to do!' said Jennifer, looking slightly aggrieved. 'I want Anna to know that it can be dreadful working in the same place as—'

'I think she's aware of that!' said Rebecca between clenched teeth.

'I don't know if it will be a problem,' said Anna. 'We're grown-up, civilised people—and we should be able to work together in a professional manner.'

'It's not as easy as you think,' persisted Jennifer.

'This boy was always popping over to my new department and—'

'Jennifer!' Rebecca glared at her. 'Shut up!'

'If it becomes a problem then I'll get another job,' said Anna.

'Why should *you* be the one to get a new job?' asked Rebecca. 'Why can't *he* move?'

Anna shook her head slowly. 'I wasn't going to go into too much detail, but I feel that if anyone moves jobs it should be me because I was the one who caused the engagement to be broken off. I didn't want to set a date for the wedding and he gave me an ultimatum. It's my fault, really. I just can't make the commitment.'

'But you loved him, didn't you?' asked Rebecca.

'Yes. I still do. And that's something I'm going to have to get over,' Anna replied.

'I got over this boy quite quickly, actually—'

'Jennifer! Shut up!' Rebecca repeated crossly. She reached out and touched Anna gently on the shoulder. 'I'm glad you came round and told us. I hope it helps you to get over it quicker, sharing it with us. And you know we're always here for you…and Mum and Dad, too. Have you told them yet?'

'No,' said Anna. 'I'm planning on calling round to see them now. At least Dad won't have another wedding to pay for!'

'Oh, my goodness—the wedding! The wedding's off!' exclaimed Jennifer, as if she'd only just fully realised the implication of her sister's broken engagement. 'How terrible! That means the twins won't be bridesmaids!'

'Jennifer!' said Rebecca, even sterner than before. 'Will you *shut up*?'

CHAPTER NINE

IT HAD been three whole weeks since the broken engagement—and Anna had seen Jack on numerous occasions at the hospital. When they'd found themselves working together he'd behaved in exactly the way she'd predicted...in a civilised and professional manner.

Anna coped with the trauma of the break-up by throwing herself into her work. She was always the first in on her shift and the last out. Filling every available second with either work or sleep helped cushion the blow—or at least stopped her dwelling too deeply on the recent past.

It was late morning in A and E and Anna decided she'd get a cup of coffee after she'd seen her next patient. The desk nurse handed her a file.

'Male patient, aged thirty, sore throat, in cubicle three,' she said, handing Anna the buff folder. 'He asked for you.'

'I wonder why?' Anna said, walking over to the examination cubicle and drawing back the curtain. A man, casually dressed but smartly so, was sitting in a chair next to the examination couch. She read his notes. She couldn't recall having dealt with him before and the name wasn't familiar.

'Mr Wilson?' she enquired, just to make sure she had the right notes.

'That's correct,' he said, rising politely from his chair. 'It's Steve. Steve Wilson.'

'Please, remain seated for the time being,' said Anna. 'I'm just checking your notes to see if you've been in A and E, or the Royal, before.'

'No, I haven't. This is my first time. I'm a Royal virgin, so to speak.' He gave a strange laugh. Anna looked up sharply.

'I was just wondering why you asked for me, that's all.'

'Oh, that!' He paused for a moment and seemed to go all shy. 'I was watching you while I was sitting in the waiting area and I asked what your name was. I liked the look of you...as a doctor, that is.'

'I see.' Anna closed the file briskly, deciding not to delve too closely into Steve Wilson's strange behaviour.

'A sore throat, is it?'

'That's right. Very sore,' he confirmed.

She removed the sterile wrapping from a tongue depressor and took the penlight from her top pocket.

'Would you just sit on the edge of the examination bed, Mr Wilson, and open your mouth for me, please?'

He smiled at her. 'Anything you say, Doctor.' He positioned himself as she'd instructed and opened his mouth.

Anna checked inside his mouth and in particular around the tonsil area for signs of infection.

'There's a small amount of redness,' she said, 'but nothing too worrying.'

She then took his temperature, which was normal, and felt around his neck for any sign of swollen lymph nodes.

'Swallow, please,' she instructed him. 'And again.' Her fingers probed gently around the thyroid gland.

She then checked the range of movement he had in his head and neck.

She dropped the disposable tongue depressor in the waste bin and returned the penlight to her top pocket.

'I think we can safely say there's nothing seriously wrong with you,' she told him as she wrote in his notes. 'I wouldn't even consider giving you antibiotics at this stage. Take some proprietary throat lozenges, which you can buy from any chemist, just to moisten the throat...and drink plenty of fluids. You'll be right as rain in a couple of days, if not sooner.' She smiled at him in a friendly manner.

He smiled back, casting his eyes over her face and then her hair and back again to her face, upon which his gaze lingered.

'Thanks, Doctor,' he said. 'You must think me a terrible hypochondriac!'

'Not at all,' said Anna, drawing back the curtain to leave.

'I just thought it's better to be safe than sorry,' he said, following her out. 'You keep hearing all the time about these life-threatening illnesses that start with a sore throat!'

'I'm sure you've nothing to worry about but, of course if it gets a lot worse, or if you have any other symptoms, then go to your GP.'

'I haven't got one at the moment,' he replied. 'I've just moved house. So is it OK if I come back here?'

'Yes, of course.'

She walked briskly away, slapping Mr Wilson's file on the desk, muttering under her breath, 'Why did I say that? I've just made a rod for my own back!'

Of course she knew why she'd said it—the last thing she wanted was for Steve Wilson to be told by her that there was nothing wrong with him, only to discover later that he was suffering from something really serious. But wasn't that the risk doctors took all the time? It was something you had to live with, as long as you'd done the best job you could possibly do at the time. Mistakes got made, she was only too aware of that. But she'd put money on Steve Wilson being, in his own words, 'a hypochondriac'. And as for asking for her by name—a patient she'd never seen before—well, that was just plain cheeky!

It was getting towards the end of Anna's shift, a shift which had been quite tiring. There'd been no adrenalin-boosting dramas—no vehicle pile-ups or chain-saw massacres—just a steady flow of cases throughout the whole shift. It meant that Anna had been on her feet the whole time. She hadn't even had time for a tea break until it was almost time for the next shift to take over.

'I'll make you a drink,' said one of the nurses as Anna leaned on the desk. 'You look parched. What'll it be, tea or coffee?'

'Coffee, milk, no sugar. Thanks, Tammy.'

'Oops, he's here again,' said Tammy softly, her eyes indicating the door that led into the A and E department. Anna turned and saw Steve Wilson walking towards her. He smiled widely.

'Hello, Doctor,' he said walking straight up to her. 'I'm so glad you're still here.'

'Mr Wilson,' said Anna, putting on a bright face. 'How's the throat?'

'Much worse,' he said, touching his neck. 'It's a good job you told me not to hesitate to come back if it got worse. I feel that you possibly had an idea that it might turn into something nasty. You did warn me.'

'I didn't mean to give that impression, Mr Wilson. If you recall, I said you probably had nothing to worry about.' She turned to Tammy. 'Can you give me Mr Wilson's file again, please? And keep the coffee for me for later. Thanks.'

Tammy riffled through the files, found the correct one and handed it to Anna. 'Cubicle two's empty,' she said.

'Would you follow me, Mr Wilson?' she said, walking towards the examination cubicle.

He followed her in and drew the curtain behind them. This action on his part made Anna feel, once again, slightly uneasy in this man's presence.

She examined his throat for the second time that afternoon. If anything, the redness was a lot less, almost non-existent. She went through the same examination procedure that she'd done earlier, this time extending it by listening to his chest and back.

'I still can't find anything wrong with you, Mr Wilson.'

'Steve, please.'

'Well, Steve, as I said, I can't find any sign of infection or disease. Have you bought anything from the chemist?'

'What kind of thing did you have in mind?' He asked the question with a hint of double meaning and a sly grin on his face.

'Throat lozenges,' she said, ignoring his attempt at humour.

'Can you write me down some names of ones you'd recommend?' he asked.

She scribbled some brand names down on a sheet of paper from a notepad and handed it to him.

'Thanks, Doctor,' he said, taking the note.

Anna walked quickly out of the cubicle and closed the curtain behind her so that he could put on his shirt in privacy...and also to distance herself from him. She was convinced he was a time-waster.

'Hi,' said a familiar voice behind her as she walked towards her car.

'Oh, Jack, hi!' she said, turning to face him. 'Busy day?'

'Not too bad,' he said, matching his stride to hers. His eyes looked sad and she longed to go to him and be held in his arms. And yet she was convinced she'd done the right thing in precipitating the break-up. How could she marry him when she was so distrustful of his motives? Nevertheless, the pain and the longing just wouldn't go away.

If Jack's eyes betrayed sadness, it was just the tip of the iceberg. He'd known a lot of sorrow in his life but this was sorrow of a different kind. It was like a knife being twisted in his side, and every time he saw Anna it was as if the knife was pushed in a little deeper. He'd finally got over losing his wife, only to find he'd now also lost the only other woman he'd ever loved.

Anna moved briskly towards her own car, keys at the ready. At that moment, out of the corner of her eye, she could see someone waving to her from across the car park. It was Steve Wilson. She gave an involuntary gasp.

'Anything the matter?' asked Jack.

'No, not really,' she said. 'It's just that man over there. He's waving to me.'

Jack looked in the direction she was pointing. 'What about him?'

'I don't know. He's a patient, a bit of a hypochondriac, I think, and...' As she spoke she realised how feeble it sounded. Was she becoming paranoid?

'Lots of patients are hypochondriacs,' said Jack. 'I wouldn't let that bother you.'

'It doesn't really.' She put her key in the lock. 'Bye, Jack.'

She drove home with a classical music station turned up loudly. Every now and then she'd check her driving mirrors because for some inexplicable reason she had the feeling that she was being followed by Steve Wilson. There was so much traffic, though, that it was hard for her to notice if any one car was tailing her all the way home. And when she reached her apartment block and drove into the underground car park she was alone. Nobody had followed her in.

'Stop being so jittery!' she told herself as she took the lift to the second floor.

'These are for you,' said Tammy, as Anna arrived at work the following day, pointing to the large bouquet of flowers that was taking up a lot of space on the triage desk.

'You must have a secret admirer,' said one of the other nurses. 'Perhaps it's Mr Harvey. Are you and he back together again?'

'Er, no,' said Anna. She went over to the flowers and picked up the card that had come with them. Her heart fluttered as she opened the tiny envelope. Could they be from Jack? She smiled in anticipation, but the smile froze on her lips as she read the words on the card.

'Thanks, Anna, for your expert medical care—and, most of all, for your personal touch. Will you have dinner with me? Steve Wilson'

'Oh, no!' she uttered in dismay.

'Anything the matter?' asked Tammy.

Anna popped the card in her pocket and pointed to the flowers. 'They're from a patient,' she said offhandedly. 'Why don't we put them in the waiting room?'

'OK,' said Tammy. 'I'll do it. I love arranging flowers and these are just gorgeous.' She picked up the flowers and breathed in the perfume. 'They must have cost a fortune.'

Later that morning Anna spied Steve Wilson again. He was walking towards her, past the waiting area and the triage desk.

'Oh, hell!' she muttered, the blood draining from her face. Why was she so nervous of this man? He was just a patient after all.

'Hi, Anna,' he said, smiling broadly and continuing to walk towards her.

'You'll have to check in at the reception desk, Mr Wilson,' said Anna, backing away from him.

He waved his hand at the two nurses on the triage desk, saying, 'I'm not a patient today, ladies. It's personal. I'm just calling in to have a quick word with Anna.'

At that moment, Jack came into the A and E and saw the man going over to Anna. He registered the way the two nurses raised their eyebrows and looked at each other—and then across to where the man and Anna were now talking.

'Is that the guy who sent Dr Craven the flowers?' he heard one of them ask the other.

'I think so,' came the reply. 'They're on first-name terms—or so it would appear!'

Jack continued walking past the triage desk and turned his gaze away from Anna. He had to accept that her private life was her own affair now. It was none of his business what she got up to or who she spoke to.

'Did you get the flowers?' Steve Wilson asked pleasantly when he reached Anna.

'Thank you,' she said. 'They're lovely. One of the nurses has put them in the waiting area. Anyway, how's the throat?'

'A lot better,' he said, tapping his pocket. 'Thanks to the lozenges you recommended. I carry them with me all the time.' He made it sound like a love token.

'Really?' said Anna. 'Why?'

'To remind me,' he said huskily, touching her lightly with one finger.

'That's a strange thing to do,' she said in a small voice.

'Did you think I meant to remind me of you?' He laughed warmly. 'I actually meant to remind me to take them! Although, of course, they remind me of you as well. So, Anna, what's the answer?'

'What's the question?'

'Will you have dinner with me?' His voice was calm and reasonable, his eyes meltingly soft.

'No, Steve,' Anna replied, adopting a similarly reasonable tone. 'It's not allowed. You're my patient. You don't want to get me struck off the medical register, do you?' She gave a small laugh.

'It's him, isn't it?' His face clouded. 'That man I saw you with in the car park. Is he your boyfriend?'

Anna cast her mind back and realised Steve was referring to the brief meeting she'd had with Jack at the end of yesterday's shift. She jumped at the opportunity this now offered her.

'Well, yes, actually,' she said. 'He's my boyfriend and that's another reason why I can't go out with you.'

'I understand,' said Steve. 'Well, so long.' He smiled and walked away, not looking back even as he opened the door leading from the A and E.

The next morning, she started up the car and reversed out of her parking space.

The car felt strange—kind of 'bumpy'. She wasn't at all mechanically minded and, after she'd driven a short distance in the underground car park, she got out to have a look to see if there was anything obvious that might be causing the car to feel so odd. She worried that it might be something to do with the steering-wheel as it seemed to be pulling in one particular direction like a wonky supermarket trolley.

As she looked at the outside of the car she discovered immediately what the problem was. She had a flat tyre.

'Damn!' she cursed. Looking at her watch, she realised that even if she knew how to change a wheel she wouldn't have time to do it. There was nobody else in the car park to talk to about her dilemma so she decided to leave the car and phone her garage when she got to work. She manoeuvred the vehicle back into its parking spot and locked it, placing the keys out of sight on top of one of the wheels.

She walked away from her apartment block towards the bus stop. If a bus didn't come in the next five minutes, she'd be seriously late for her shift. She also phoned for a cab, but at this hour of the morning she couldn't be sure of one being available straight away. It was all very annoying. If only she'd known she was going to have a flat tyre she would have set off for work half an hour earlier!

Anna was waiting at the bus stop, just about to phone the hospital to warn them that she'd be late, when a car pulled up and a man called out of the open window.

'Are you waiting for a lift?' he said.

A wave of relief washed over her and she put her mobile away. No need to phone the hospital after all! But as she walked towards the car she realised with dismay that it wasn't the private hire cab after all. It was Steve Wilson.

'I thought you were my taxi,' she said, stepping back onto the pavement.

'I was just passing and saw you at the bus stop. Don't you usually drive to the hospital?' he asked genially.

'I've got a puncture,' she said.

'Would you like me to change the wheel for you?' His face was eager and guileless.

'No, thanks,' said Anna brusquely. 'My garage will sort it out.'

'Let me give you a lift into work, then,' he said, getting out of his car and walking over to her.

'It's OK,' she said. 'I've called a taxi.'

He looked around the deserted road.

'No bus and no taxi in sight,' he remarked. 'Come on,' he said, picking up Anna's bag and walking towards his own car. 'I'm going that way myself so I might as well drop you off.' He put her bag on the back seat and opened the front passenger door for her.

Reluctantly she got into the car. There was something very creepy about this man but she couldn't quite decide what it was. To have refused his offer of a lift in these circumstances would only have made her look ridiculous.

'Thanks,' she said, fastening her seat belt and staring straight ahead.

She was grateful that the radio was switched on as, even though the music wasn't to her liking, it meant she didn't feel obliged to make small talk with him.

He didn't seem to want to talk either. It was only when they reached the hospital that he spoke.

'I can arrange to have your tyre mended and then bring your car along to the hospital for you to have at the end of your shift. Would you like me to do that for you?' He was smiling warmly at her. It sent a shiver down her spine.

'No, thanks, Steve,' she said. 'It's really very kind of you and very kind of you to give me a lift, but I've already phoned my garage.'

Anna hadn't phoned the garage yet, but she wasn't going to admit that to him. He was very persistent and, no doubt, would have insisted on changing the wheel, given half the chance.

She picked up her bag from the back seat and glanced at his face again. He seemed genuine enough, smiling happily even though she knew she was being very frosty towards him. Perhaps she was overreacting? He had, after all, saved her from being late for her shift and she was grateful for that.

'Thanks again,' she said, smiling at him, 'and

thanks for offering to change the wheel. It might not need changing, of course. It could be that all it needs is pumping up...I didn't think about that at the time!'

'I don't think so,' he said in a quiet voice.

'What?'

'I don't think it needed pumping up.' He put his car into gear and drove away.

What a strange thing to say, she thought. It's almost as if he'd known about her flat tyre before she did! And how odd that he should just happen to turn up outside her apartment at that precise moment. She shivered, telling herself not to be paranoid. There was probably a perfectly simple explanation for everything.

The next day, Tammy came into the trauma room and said to the assembled group of medics, 'I've got a drugs overdose, a man with angina, a broken nose and a blocked bowel.' She handed out the files to each of them in turn. As she gave Anna her file she added, 'And a large bunch of flowers is waiting in Reception for you.'

'For me? Are you sure?' Anna was disbelieving.

'Don't look so shocked,' said Tammy. 'It's only a bunch of flowers—not the Grim Reaper!'

Anna marched into Reception and saw the flowers on the triage desk. She picked up the spray and read the attached card.

'Glad to be of assistance, Anna. Any time, anywhere. Steve'

She was now beginning to get angry with this man. He was definitely a nutter! She strode up to a tall rubbish bin and shoved the flowers into it, tearing up the card into tiny pieces dropping them on top of the flowers like confetti. As she was doing this, Jack walked past.

'Got a new job as flower monitor?' he asked.

'No,' she said. 'Just a crazy man who keeps sending me flowers.'

'I'd no idea you had a flower phobia!' replied Jack, walking away, his heart leaden. Was there another man in her life so soon after their break-up? The possibility didn't bear thinking about and he pushed it to the back of his mind.

Alex, the junior doctor, heard the exchange between Anna and Jack.

'What's going on?' he asked. 'That's a very odd thing to do with a nice bunch of flowers.'

'Odd is precisely what it is,' said Anna tensely. 'They're from a very odd patient and I'm probably overreacting—but if he sends me any more they're going to end up in the bin also.'

'Who's the patient?' Alex asked. 'We'll look out for him in future.'

'He's called Steve Wilson,' said Anna resignedly. 'I'm beginning to think he's stalking me! He's making me nervous and jumpy and yet there's nothing specific I can point to and say he's becoming a threat...nothing I can go to the police with at any rate.'

Anna's hands were trembling as she picked up the patient file. Alex noticed how much she was shaking.

'I feel so silly,' she said. 'What's wrong with me?'

'Tell me about this Steve Wilson,' said Alex. 'What's he actually done?'

Anna sighed. 'Nothing really. That's the whole point. He's not doing anything threatening—and yet he makes me feel threatened. He's been in A and E a couple of times with a bogus illness...he said he had a very bad sore throat and yet there was nothing much to see. Then he sent me flowers, twice. The first time he asked me out to dinner, and then this morning when my car had a flat tyre he mysteriously appeared and offered me a lift to work.'

'And that's it?' he said.

She nodded.

'How does he know where you live?' asked Alex.

'I don't know,' said Anna, 'but a couple of nights ago, when I was driving home, I had the feeling that I was being followed. Do you think I'm overreacting?'

'I wouldn't say you were overreacting,' said Alex, 'but perhaps he only wants to get to know you better and doesn't realise he's being a pest. If he's upsetting you—and he obviously is—then he's got to stop it. Let me know if anything else happens and we can alert Security.'

'Thanks, Alex.' She picked up her file. 'I'd better go and unblock this bowel.'

The next morning, Anna was in early for her shift and was relaxing, chatting to Tammy and Alex, when one of the receptionists from the main hospital desk walked in, carrying a large bunch of flowers.

'The young man said you'd know who they were from,' said the receptionist, 'but I made him tell me his name anyway.' She checked what was written on the scrap of paper she was holding. 'He said he was Steve Wilson.'

Jack had just walked into the room and saw the look on Anna's face as she was handed the bouquet.

'Is this from the man who sent them before?' he asked, trying to keep the hurt out of his voice.

'I'm afraid so,' said Anna, 'and I'm going to dispose of them in exactly the same way.' She flung the flowers into the nearest bin.

'That's a shame,' said Tammy. 'They're lovely flowers. Are they from your handsome friend, the gentleman patient who asks for you by name?'

Before Anna could answer, Jack said, 'They're from a patient? I didn't know you'd become emotionally involved with a patient. That's really not a good idea, Anna.'

Anna, whose face had blanched when she'd been handed the flowers, now felt the blood rushing to her cheeks. 'I'm not emotionally involved with him!' she blazed.

Jack put up his hands. 'If you say so! But you seem pretty emotional about him at the moment!' He turned his back on her and walked out of the room. He didn't want to stay any longer to find out the sordid details of Anna's latest romantic entanglement. And with a patient! She really ought to know better.

A few moments later, Alex caught up with him in the corridor.

'Jack,' he said, 'I think I ought to tell you something.'

The two men faced each other. 'Yes, what is it?' asked Jack.

'Those flowers that were sent to Anna. They're not from a boyfriend, as you seem to be assuming.'

'Oh? And how would you know? Anna confides in you now, does she, about her love life? I very much doubt that someone as private as Anna would do that.'

He made as if to go, annoyed that Alex was muscling in on things. He needed to mind his own business!

'He's a nutter,' said Alex. 'He's been pestering Anna for days and it's bordering on harassment. I've even alerted the hospital security team. She's extremely upset about it and she looked devastated when you got the wrong end of the story. I just wanted to let you know.'

'Oh!' said Jack, chastened. Now he felt bad, and more than a little guilty, for having said the things he had to Anna. 'Thanks, Alex, for putting me in the picture.' He also admitted to himself that the main reason he'd reacted so harshly was that he was jealous. Jealous that she might be involved with another man.

As he walked back to his office, Jack experienced a mixture of emotions. Anger that someone would upset Anna in such a way, concern that it might continue and get worse—and relief that she hadn't taken up with a new man.

Anna was finding it very hard to concentrate on her work that day. The incident with the flowers and the confrontation with Jack had unsettled her. She became nervous about going into the patients' waiting area in case Steve was there.

By the time the end of her shift was in sight and he hadn't shown up, Anna was able to breathe more calmly and relax a little. Alex had been a tower of strength, telling her that he'd alerted Security and the staff on both reception desks, informing them that they shouldn't allow Steve Wilson into the A and E department.

She took off her soiled white coat and put it in the

laundry shute before putting on her own jacket in readiness to leave.

'Bye, everyone,' she said on her way out. 'See you tomorrow.'

Her relaxed mood was short-lived. Standing in the car park next to her car was Steve Wilson. If she'd noticed him earlier she would have gone straight back into the hospital and called Security. But she didn't notice him until she was almost at her vehicle. He must have been standing in the shadows, only revealing himself when she was almost level with him.

'Oh!' she said, startled.

'Hi, Anna,' he said. 'Did you get the flowers?'

His voice was calm and reasonable and not in the least threatening—but nevertheless it made her shake all over. She was holding her car keys and could hear them jangling together. She wondered if he could also hear the noise. She desperately hoped he couldn't because the last thing she wanted was for him to know that she was afraid.

'Yes, I got the flowers, Steve, but I really don't want you to send me any more. I hate flowers, you see. I'm allergic to them.' She glanced swiftly around the badly lit car park and realised to her dismay that there was no one else around. She managed to get the key in the lock despite her shaky hand.

'I'm sorry about that,' said Steve, leaning on her car door and preventing her from opening it. 'I won't send any more.'

'Good,' said Anna brightly. 'Do you mind letting me open my car door, please?'

'I was wondering if you'd give me a lift home,' he said. 'My car's got a flat tyre, just like yours had. Funny old world, isn't it?' He was smiling, his face so close to hers that she could smell his rancid breath. 'It would be a friendly thing to do, to repay my favour of yesterday, wouldn't it?'

Anna felt extremely vulnerable and frightened...all the more so because he was acting so *normally*.

'I'm not going home right now—I'm still on shift,' she said. 'I've only come out to get something from my car.' She made a pretence of looking on the passenger seat. 'It's not here,' she said. 'The thing I came out for. I'd better be getting back or they'll be wondering where I am.'

She walked away quickly, hoping desperately that he wasn't following her. She cast a brief look over her shoulder and noticed, thankfully, that he was still in the same position she'd left him, leaning against her car.

She ran the last few metres to the hospital and, rushing into the main entrance, bumped straight into Jack.

'Whoa!' he said. 'Steady on!' He could see in an instant that she was distressed and immediately put his arms around her. Her whole body was shaking and he had to hold her firmly to stop her from collapsing to the ground.

'What is it, angel?' he said softly.

'It's that man, Steve Wilson!' she sobbed.

'The one who's been sending flowers?'

'Yes.' She gulped. 'He's waiting outside near my car!'

Jack reacted to this news like a pouncing tiger.

'Show me where,' he said, taking Anna by the hand as he rushed towards the entrance.

'He's probably gone by now,' she said, 'and then you'll say I've made it all up!'

Jack, stung by her accusation, paused for a moment and put his arms around her again, kissing her on the cheek.

'I'm sorry, Anna, for saying what I did this morning. Until Alex told me, I'd no idea you were being harassed by this man.'

The two of them went out into the car park and Anna pointed to her car.

'Oh, lord!' she said. 'He's still there. He's waiting for me to come back!'

Jack sprinted across the tarmac and when he reached Steve he grabbed him by the lapels and pushed him against Anna's car.

'Get the hell out of here while you can,' Jack snarled at him angrily. 'If I see you anywhere near this hospital ever again, I'll make sure you'll be needing the services of a funeral director, not a doctor! Is that clear?'

'I've done nothing wrong!' protested Wilson. 'You can't have me arrested!'

'I'm not planning on having you arrested. I'm planning on stopping you from harassing Dr Craven.'

Steve laughed in his face. 'Oh, I get it! You're her boyfriend, aren't you? You're just trying to impress her with this strong-arm stuff!'

Jack shook him, almost lifting him off his feet. 'For your information, I am *not* her boyfriend. But that doesn't mean I won't carry out my threat.'

'I could have *you* arrested for assault!' Steve's face had become hard, his voice mean.

'Be my guest,' said Jack, slowly releasing his grip. 'I look forward to seeing you in court.' He let go of Wilson and took two paces back. He pointed to the car-park exit. 'Get out!'

Steve made an exaggerated show of brushing himself down and straightening his jacket before walking away. He didn't look in Anna's direction, she was glad to note.

When he was sure that Steve had left, Jack took Anna back inside the hospital entrance. 'I hope that's the last we'll hear from Mr Wilson,' he said, putting a comforting arm around her.

'Thanks, Jack,' said Anna. 'I'm very grateful to you.' She buried her head in his shoulder. 'I don't know what's come over me, I'm a bundle of nerves...and the silly thing is that I don't know if the guy really is crazy or just has a crush on me.'

'It would be understandable if he had a crush on you,' said Jack, breathing in her perfume and glad of the excuse to hold her close for that little bit longer. 'You have to accept that you're a very beautiful and desirable woman. His actions could be interpreted in a different way if you look at them in that context.'

'But he makes me so nervous!'

'And that's why he has to be stopped. I may have gone over the top with him just now but I wanted to put the frighteners on him.'

'I think you did that!' said Anna. 'Just watching you from a safe distance made me feel quite scared on his behalf!'

'I was only giving him a dose of his own medicine.' He kissed her on the top of her head and reluctantly removed his arm from around her shoulders. 'Security are on the lookout for him in the vicinity of the hospital so you'll be safe when you're at work. And he doesn't know where you live.'

'He does!' said Anna, tensing up again. 'I think he

followed me home one evening and yesterday he saw me outside my apartment on the way to work.'

Jack didn't want to destroy Anna's new-found hope that the situation was under control. 'I'm sure you'll have no more trouble with him. He doesn't look the dangerous type, just a sad, lonely, pathetic man who has trouble forming relationships.'

'Yes,' said Anna, 'I'm sure you're right... But would you walk me to my car just this once? I'm still a bit jittery.'

'I'll give you a phone call when I get home,' said Jack, walking with her, 'just to make sure you're OK.'

'Thanks,' she said, reaching up and kissing him on the cheek. 'You're a real friend in need.' She got into her car and Jack watched her drive away.

'I don't want to be your *friend*, Anna!' he muttered aloud.

Clenching his fists, he walked back to the hospital to finish writing up his notes before leaving for home.

CHAPTER TEN

Anna drove home with the radio on a popular music station. She sang along to the songs in an effort to lift her spirits and calm her nerves.

It worked, and by the time she parked her car in her underground parking space she was feeling much more composed and in control. Perhaps it was the way Jack had rallied round, sending Steve packing.

She'd missed Jack so much in the weeks since their engagement had been broken off. Of course, she saw him at work but that wasn't the same thing as having him holding her in his arms. She could still feel his strong embrace from a few minutes earlier when he'd calmed her down and kissed her on the cheek. He was a tower of strength and she was so glad they could still remain friends—if nothing else.

She was turning these thoughts over in her mind as she walked up the two flights of stairs to her apartment. Even after a day's work she often preferred to walk rather than take the lift. Only on the days when she was totally exhausted would she choose the easy option.

On reaching her flat, she put the key in the door—and was surprised to find it unlocked.

'How strange,' she murmured to herself. 'I must have forgotten to lock it this morning.'

Shutting the door behind her and locking it from the inside, she walked into the main room and got the fright of her life. Sitting on her sofa, as cool as a cucumber, was Steve. He was smiling at her.

'Hi, Anna,' he said. 'I wondered if you'd like me to cook you a meal tonight, with you having worked such a long shift.'

Anna's first instinct was to run for the door, but as she made a move, Steve stood up. She realised with a sinking heart that, because she'd locked the door, it would take a few moments to unlock it again before she could escape. And, as this man was obviously crazy, the best option might be to try and reason with him in a calm manner.

'Don't leave!' he said, walking over to her.

'I'm not,' she said in as reassuring a voice as she could muster. 'I'm just putting my jacket in the hall.' Thinking quickly, she added, 'It's not really convenient for you to cook me a meal tonight because I've arranged to go out with someone. I'm just going to check that he's ready, so I'll make a quick phone call...'

She moved slowly towards the telephone, making her actions as casual as possible.

'Is this "someone" the man who says he's not your boyfriend, but who you say *is* your boyfriend?' Steve asked, an ugly expression replacing the smile on his face.

'Er, I'm not sure what you're talking about,' said Anna, almost at the phone, her eyes not leaving him. He made no attempt to stop her from picking it up. When she placed the instrument to her ear she knew why. The line was dead. She looked down and saw the cord had been cut.

A most terrible fear gripped her. She put the phone down slowly.

'What's the matter?' Steve asked, his voice hard and triumphant.

'The phone's not working,' she said, backing away from him.

'That's a shame,' he said. 'Would you like me to fix it for you? I used to work in that kind of business and I'm very good with my hands.'

'No, thanks.' A rush of adrenalin emboldened her, making her feel more able to stand up to him. 'What I'd like to know is how you got into my flat. Is breaking and entering part of your work experience as well?'

Steve laughed. It was that same strange laugh that she'd noticed when she'd first met him in A and E. 'What do you think?' he asked. 'I think you just forgot to lock your door this morning when you left at seven thirty-eight.'

He knows the exact time I left for work! He's been watching me, checking my movements, creeping up to my flat when he knows I'm out! And cutting my telephone line!

'I see,' she said, moving quickly to the door. She managed to unlock it, but he was one step behind her, grabbing her, his arm around her neck. He dragged her back into the room.

'I don't think you do see, Anna,' he said. 'You've lied to me, haven't you?' He gave her a shake, pulling her even closer to his body and hurting her throat.

'I haven't lied!' she protested.

'You told me that he was your boyfriend—that bully-boy doctor who roughed me up in the car park!'

He shook her again, like a rag doll. His arm was so tightly pressed against her neck that she could hardly breathe, let alone answer him.

'Your bully-boy doctor told me a different story,' he went on. 'He said that he *wasn't* your boyfriend! So what am I to make of that, Anna?' He shook her again and she felt in danger of losing consciousness. His grip was so strong that all she could think was that it was true what they said about the strength of maniacs.

'I think you lied to me for one of two reasons,' he said, his mouth close to her ear, his hot breath searing her skin. 'Either you find me so repulsive that you can't bear me near you...or you find me very attractive and want to play hard to get.' He gave that strange laugh again and loosened his grip slightly. She let herself go limp, deciding that it was the struggling that had made him grip her so tightly. 'Do you find me repulsive, Anna?'

'No,' she said weakly, terrified of increasing his anger.

'Good,' he said softly. 'That means you're just playing hard to get.'

She began to struggle again, realising the implication of what she'd said.

'I'm not!' she tried to say, but he'd put his hand over her mouth to prevent any more words spilling out.

'I like a woman with spirit,' he said, dragging her over to the sofa. 'It makes the sexual act so much more enjoyable, don't you think, Anna? But don't bother struggling any more because I've got a knife. I don't want to use it...unless you make me.'

There was a banging on the door and she heard Jack's voice calling out, 'Are you all right, Anna?'

With a superhuman effort she clawed at Steve's

hand, pulling it from her mouth, and yelled at the top of her voice, '*Help!*'

Instantaneously, Jack flung open the door and hurled himself at Anna's attacker, wrestling him to the floor.

'He's got a knife,' screamed Anna as she saw the glint of a blade.

Jack grabbed Steve's wrist, forcing him to drop the knife, but not before the maniac had plunged it twice into Jack. Blood poured from his wounds as the two men rolled over and over on Anna's floor. Sometimes it appeared that Jack had the upper hand, at other times it was Steve.

The fight went on for what seemed to Anna an extremely long time but was probably not more than a few minutes. At one point, when Steve was on top of Jack, his fist raised to punch Jack in the face, Anna managed to grapple with him and deflect the blow. Steve, who seemed to have remarkable strength for his build, lashed back with his fist and struck Anna in the face, cutting her lip.

Her intervention, however, had given Jack a momentary advantage and he managed to swing Steve round again, forcing him down against the carpet.

'Get the knife!' Jack shouted to Anna when he saw Steve's hand reaching out to retrieve his weapon. She wasn't quick enough and in a flash he'd picked up the knife and plunged it into Jack's shoulder.

The men continued to struggle, with Anna intervening when possible by kicking and clawing at Steve, who still had the knife in his hand. Jack swung him over on his back again and Anna saw her chance as the knife was knocked out of Steve's hand. She grabbed it, but when she saw the blood on it and felt the stickiness in her hand, she threw it to the far side of the room in horror and disgust.

She had intended to use it against Steve but she just couldn't...though she knew she had to do something quickly to stop the fight, which now looked as if it would end in the death of one of the men. As she watched Steve's hands go round Jack's throat she screamed, 'Stop it! Stop it!'

In desperation she cast around the room for a weapon. Her eyes came to rest on a table lamp which had a marble base. She picked it up, yanking it from its electric cord, and held it over the two men, waiting for an opportunity to hit the right one. It wasn't easy because both of them were so closely entwined that it was impossible to find any space between them.

Jack, in a supreme effort, managed to pull Steve's hands from his throat and push him sufficiently away for Anna to hit Steve with the table lamp. Because the men were constantly moving, she didn't make a direct hit the first time, just a glancing blow. She tried again and this time the marble base made contact with Steve's head, knocking him out cold.

As he went limp, so did Jack who slumped to the ground next to Steve's unconscious body.

'Are you all right?' she asked in consternation. 'I'll phone an ambulance...'

'Yes, but tie him up first.' Jack's voice was barely audible.

'What? Oh, I see what you mean...in case he wakes up?' She ran into the kitchen, frantically opening cupboards.

'I haven't got a rope!' she said, knowing that it would be only by a miracle that she would find a convenient length of rope lying in wait for just such an emergency.

'Electric flex,' called out Jack.

'Oh, yes!' She ran back into the living room and over to where she'd pulled out the lamp from the wall. A long length of flex was still attached to a plug in the wall socket. Even in her state of panic she had the presence of mind to switch off the socket before removing the plug and its useful length of strong electrical cable.

She ran with it to where the two men were still lying on the blood-splattered carpet. It was only then that she realised Jack hadn't moved from the position in which she'd left him. His eyes were closed, a deathly pallor on his face.

'Oh, Jack, speak to me!' She felt his pulse, trying to establish how badly he was injured. His eyes flickered open.

'I've got some quite deep wounds,' he said, 'and I think I'm bleeding internally because I'm feeling very light-headed... Blood pressure dropping...'

Through gasping breaths he continued, 'Just get the bastard tied up... then call the police... and an ambulance... Use my mobile phone... Do it quickly...'

She secured the flex around Steve's hands and feet, tying him so firmly that even if he did regain full consciousness, there would be little he could do about it.

While they were waiting for the police and ambulance, Anna knelt down next to Jack. He managed to pull himself up on one elbow.

'You're safe,' he said to her, feeling the trembling of her body. 'He can't get you now.'

She looked at the senseless body of her attacker.

'Thank heavens you came,' she said.

'I tried your phone, but it was out of order... I began to worry,' said Jack.

'He cut the wire,' she said numbly.

They continued to stare at the still unconscious Steve.

'Do you think I've killed him?' said Anna.

'Let's hope so,' said Jack.

They were the last words he uttered before he, too, slipped into unconsciousness—just at the moment the ambulance crew arrived.

Three days had passed and Jack's condition had improved dramatically. He was now out of Intensive Care where he'd been moved after spending four hours in the operating theatre. His internal injuries had resulted in a massive blood loss but transfusions, expert nursing and his own robust constitution had proved more than a match for the damage inflicted on him by Steve Wilson.

Ironically, the two men had spent the first twenty-four hours in adjacent intensive-care beds following surgery. When Steve was considered to be out of danger, he was moved to a secure room in the psychiatric ward. A police officer was stationed outside, waiting to take a statement when the medical staff gave him the go-ahead.

Anna, who'd kept a vigil at Jack's bedside, decided that once he was out of danger she'd briefly leave the hospital for a change of clothes and a soak in a hot bath. She took a taxi to her parents' apartment, unable to face going back to her own. In the aftermath of the attack, her family had been magnificent, putting themselves at her disposal and doing everything they could to make the situation more bearable.

Her sisters had organised the cleaning of Anna's apartment. The heavily blood-stained carpet was considered to be irretrievable and was replaced with a new one. Ted had organised everything with the insurance company. Superficial damage was repaired by Neil, who was a dab hand at DIY. He also changed the locks, fitting new ones. A specialist cleaning company was employed to give the flat a thorough once-over to remove any traces of the horrendous events that had taken place.

Jennifer and Rebecca filled a suitcase with some of Anna's clothes and took it, along with Anna's car, to their parents' home. Mr and Mrs Craven had made up the bed in the spare bedroom, anticipating that their daughter would probably not be happy living alone in her own apartment for the time being.

'I feel so much better after that!' said Anna, coming out of the bathroom in her robe and drying her hair on a towel. She sank down in the comfortable chintzy sofa.

'Would you like that cup of coffee now?' her mother asked.

'Yes, please, Mum.' Anna continued rubbing her hair on the towel. 'I feel so relaxed and refreshed. I was beginning to think I'd never get clean again. Three days is a long time to go without a proper wash!'

'Couldn't you have had a shower at the hospital?' asked her mother. 'I'm surprised no one suggested that to you, dear.'

'They did, but I didn't want to leave Jack's bedside

for a moment. I wanted to be the first person he'd see when he woke up. And then when he did wake up I just wanted to sit with him, holding his hand. It was only when I was assured that he was definitely out of danger that I trusted myself to leave him for a short while.'

Anna took a sip of the coffee, clasping the mug in both hands.

'Would you like to borrow my hair-dryer?' her mother asked, noticing that Anna's hair was still quite wet.

'Yes, please. Now that my hair's shorter, it takes no time at all to blow-dry it.'

'Well, I suppose there must be some compensation,' said her mother, scrutinising Anna's face.

'What do you mean, compensation?'

'You must admit, darling, that this short, dark style doesn't suit you as much as the long, blonde one.' Mrs Craven could see that she'd put her daughter on the defensive and raised her hand in a gesture of peace. 'I *know* you had a good reason for doing it...all that business about being mistaken for Jack's first wife...but you only have to look in the mirror to realise that it's not really *you*.'

Anna was definitely on the defensive.

'What do you mean, *not really me*? Of course it is!'

Mrs Craven sat next to Anna and put a comforting arm around her. 'You haven't got the right skin tone or eye colour to go with that dark hair, that's all I'm saying. Rebecca and Jennifer and I all have hazel eyes. Yours are pale green. They're beautiful and unusual and they were *meant* to go with your natural blonde hair. Don't think I'm criticising you, love.

You can do exactly what you want with your appearance. That's your privilege, but it's my privilege as a mother to speak my mind!' She gave her daughter a hug. 'I just hope it worked, that's all.'

'What do you mean?' Anna looked puzzled.

'Well, you did say that you were doing it to test Jack...to see if he still loved you when you no longer looked like Anneka.'

Anna leaned back against the sofa and dropped her voice. 'Oh, yes, you're right. I'd completely forgotten about all that with this Steve Wilson thing. It all seems rather pointless now.'

'I'll go and get that hair-dryer,' said her mother, sensing that Anna was becoming morose.

When she returned, Anna was still looking downcast.

'These terrible events have at least proved one thing beyond doubt,' said her mother, plugging in the hair-dryer and handing it to Anna.

Anna looked up, her face pale with dark rings round her eyes from lack of sleep and her lip still swollen from where she'd been cut.

'What has been proved?' she asked.

'That Jack loves you more than life itself. Why else would he risk his own to save yours?'

An hour later, just as Anna was getting ready to return to the hospital to be with Jack, the telephone rang. It was the police with some interesting news.

'We checked the police computer records,' said the officer, 'and, surprise, surprise, our friend Steve Wilson has been using a false name. We tracked him down through a DNA sample and he is, in fact, Christopher Crowsky, a criminal with a record as long as your arm. There's an arrest warrant out for him in Leeds for stalking, kidnap and rape.'

'Oh, God!' said Anna, feeling faint.

'We'll be taking Mr Crowsky straight from hospital to a prison cell at the first opportunity and that's where he'll be staying until his trial. There won't be a court or a judge in the country that will grant bail to this wretched man, I can assure you, Dr Craven. You can sleep soundly in your bed from now on.'

It was three weeks before Jack was allowed home from hospital. He and Anna then spent a week in a small cottage belonging to Ted and Rebecca in the hills above Coniston Water in the Lake District.

'I hope Saskia doesn't mind me taking her daddy away for a few days' recuperation,' Anna said as they drove north up the motorway.

'I've told her we'll bring her a new fluffy toy lamb,' said Jack. 'That kept her happy. And also, because my parents are up, staying in my house, she knows she'll be spoiled to death in my absence.'

Those days alone in the cottage amid the beautiful Lakeland fells were an absolute joy to them. The weather was glorious and there wasn't even a hint of the all-too-familiar misty drizzle that often shrouded this particularly scenic part of Britain.

'This is just the kind of recuperation I'd recommend for all my patients,' said Jack one morning.

They were walking along one of the footpaths that skirted the shimmering waters of the lake. Anna stopped to adjust the laces of her walking boots.

'I agree,' she said. 'This beats a bottle of antidepressants any day!'

They leaned against a stone wall in the warm late

morning sunshine. Jack slipped an arm round her shoulders.

'You know we've got to talk about this,' he said, out of the blue.

'About Coniston, or about antidepressants?' she asked. 'I love the first and don't need the second,' she jested.

He didn't say anything but she could feel the increased pressure of his arm as he pulled her close to him.

'What is it, Jack?' she asked. 'What do you want to talk about?' *As if I don't know!*

There was one subject that hadn't been broached since the trauma of the Steve Wilson attack. They'd discussed virtually everything except the one most important subject that was on both their minds. It was as if each of them was scared of what the other might say.

'Our future,' he said. 'Have we got one? Or are we destined to be just good friends, as they say?' A look of desperation had come into his eyes. 'Helping me to recuperate is one thing...but it's not going to help me in the long run. My visible wounds are healing nicely—it's the invisible ones that are causing me the most pain. Anna, I need to know...one way or the other... I need to know if...'

'I was a fool,' said Anna. 'A fool ever to have doubted you.'

'Have all your doubts gone now?' he asked, not daring to hope too much. He'd gone through such bleak times that he wasn't going to jump to any conclusions. He wasn't going to risk having his heart broken yet again.

Anna bit her lip, knowing that he wanted her to spell everything out for him.

'I love you, Jack,' she said. 'I love you more than anything—and I always did. I was just too stupid to see it!'

'And we'll get married as soon as possible?'

'As soon as possible.'

The change that came over him was remarkable. His desperation turned to elation as he picked her up and swung her round, holding her so tightly it took her breath away.

'Oh, my love,' he said, his voice ragged with emotion, 'how I've longed to hear you say that. I know you thought I was rushing things—and that's why we had that dreadful row. But I've learned to my cost that happiness can't be taken for granted. I now realise how quickly things can change and how each moment is so precious. We mustn't waste a second of it.'

He stood her on her feet and, cupping her face in his hands, kissed her with hungry intensity, heat flaming between them.

'I thought I'd lost you,' he said, his hot lips finding hers again.

A tear trickled down her cheek.

'Are you crying, my love?' he asked, kissing the salty wetness.

'I thought I'd lost you, too,' she whispered, barely able to speak the words. 'I thought he was going to kill you... Oh, Jack, I couldn't have lived without you!' She flung herself deeper into the comfort of his arms, her body aching with love for him.

'Oh, him,' said Jack dismissively. 'The only good

thing he did was to bring us back together. In a perverse way I suppose I should be grateful to him.'

They walked back to the cottage hand in hand, their hearts bursting with happiness. He loved her, she loved him—and the world was a wonderful place.

'I'm thinking of going back to my original hair colour,' Anna said later that evening when they were sitting in the cottage in front of a log fire.

Jack had a guarded expression on his face.

'I'm not saying anything about your hair colour,' he said. 'Look at the trouble it got me into last time!'

'This has nothing to do with you,' she said, kissing him on the cheek. 'It's a girl thing. I've just decided that dark brown hair doesn't suit my skin tone. Something my mother mentioned—and I think she's probably right.'

'Your mother could be right,' said Jack, grinning, 'but I couldn't possibly comment.'

'Anyway,' continued Anna, 'I'm going to start washing it out—the hair colour, I mean. Kieran told me that these semi-permanent dyes take sixteen washes to wash out.'

'That's very precise,' said Jack, 'but who's Kieran?'

Anna smiled knowingly. 'Oh, he's just a tall, dark, handsome man...who happens to be...'

'Who happens to be what?' Jack didn't like the sound of this at all.

Seeing his furrowed brow, she burst out laughing.

'Oh, Jack! Kieran's my hairdresser!'

'Er...yes, that's who I thought he must be.' He stared at her for a few moments, running his fingers through her dark curls. 'Sixteen washes, eh?'

'That's right.'

'Why don't we start right away?'

'We?' Anna caught the sexy glint in his eye and felt the familiar flames of desire for him begin to flare into life.

He raised one eyebrow provocatively.

'I thought you might need a little assistance in the shower.' He started to unbutton his shirt. 'If it's going to take sixteen shampoo sessions, let's start now.'

EPILOGUE

SIX weeks later—and restored to her natural hair colour—Anna walked down the aisle with Jack.

Her three small bridesmaids almost—but not quite—stole the show, looking, as they did, like three adorable little angels. The young pageboys, in miniature morning suits, were also greatly admired by all—but most of all by their doting parents, Ted and Rebecca.

As Anna walked out of the church, her arm linked in Jack's, the phrase 'the happy couple' came to mind and she realised what a very apt expression it was. She truly had never felt happier or more contented in her life. Jack appeared to mirror her own emotions as he beamed happily at his bride and at those around them.

Everyone, it seemed, was smiling just as happily as the newly-weds. Even Christine, who had once dreamed of becoming Mrs Jack Harvey, had accepted some time ago that it would never happen and was now delighted that her adored employer had made a good choice of bride.

Jennifer and Rebecca, who apparently had been vying with each other to see who could wear the largest, most outrageous hat, looked positively jubilant. Jack's mother, radiant in a stunning wedding outfit that she'd bought from the best dress shop in Truro, seemed overjoyed that her son had at last found true happiness. Jack's father's mind began to wander during the service as he made plans for a small extension to their house in Cornwall for when Jack, Anna and Saskia came to stay for visits or holidays.

Among Mr and Mrs Craven's wedding guests were all their friends from the sixtieth birthday party—with the exception of Bill Stone. Anna's mother had told her with wide eyes that Irene had discovered that her husband was a serial bigamist with two 'wives' and sundry children in Australia and had sent him packing. Irene was at the wedding looking defiantly glamorous, and years younger than her age, in a fabulous figure-hugging suit. She winked at Anna as she went past. It made Anna giggle and reminded her to make a mental note to beware of men called Bill Stone.

She looked at Jack, her wonderful and heroic husband. He was, like her, smiling his head off.

Modern Romance™
...seduction and
passion guaranteed

Tender Romance™
...love affairs that
last a lifetime

Sensual Romance™
...sassy, sexy and
seductive

Blaze Romance™
...the temperature's
rising

Medical Romance™
...medical drama on
the pulse

Historical Romance™
...rich, vivid and
passionate

27 new titles every month.

With all kinds of Romance for every kind of mood...

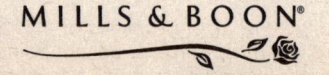

MILLS & BOON®

MILLS & BOON®

Medical Romance™

DEAR DOCTOR by Meredith Webber

Kirsten is engaged – sort of – to handsome rancher Grant. So what if playboy paediatrician Josh Phillips broke her heart? She's over it – and over him. Kirsten wants commitment, the one thing Josh can't give her. So why has her engagement done nothing at all for Kirsten's heart...and punched a hole in Josh's?

SURGEON ON CALL by Alison Roberts

Joe Petersen is a skilled surgeon – unfortunately, when it comes to being a dad he's a complete amateur! Joe's working with emergency consultant Fliss Munroe, and he wants her to be more than a colleague. What better way to get her interest than to recruit her to plan the best ever birthday party for a five-year-old girl!

THE DOCTOR'S ADOPTION WISH
by Gill Sanderson

When Nurse Jane Hall returns from California to help Dr Cal Mitchell take care of their orphaned niece, his life, his plans and his emotions are thrown into disarray. Jane might be a wanderer at heart, but Keldale is her home – and if Cal could only admit that he's fallen in love with her she just might stay for ever...

On sale 7th February 2003

Available at most branches of WH Smith, Tesco, Martins, Borders, Eason, Sainsbury's and all good paperback bookshops.

MILLS & BOON

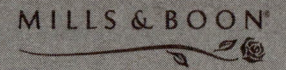

Medical Romance™

DR MICHAELIS'S SECRET by Margaret Barker

An emergency rescue on Ceres Island has recent arrival Staff Nurse Sara Metcalfe working with local doctor Michaelis Stangos – and from the moment she sees him diving into the waves she's hooked. But Sarah senses he's hiding a painful secret. A secret that's holding him back from what could be a perfect relationship...

THE FAMILY PRACTITIONER by Leah Martyn

Life is pretty uneventful for Joanne, working at the local clinic – until her teenage son Jason comes home with an outrageous request that sends Joanna marching off to see just what Dr Matthew McKellar is up to! Suddenly her life is in chaos. She's got a new job, with Matt as her new boss – and as her new lover...

HER CONSULTANT BOSS by Joanna Neil

Dr Megan Llewellyn couldn't work out what she felt most for her boss, consultant Sam Benedict – exasperation or desire! Was he hiding an attraction to her that was as intense as hers for him? When a fire destroyed her home and Megan found herself living with Sam she quickly found her answer!

On sale 7th February 2003

Available at most branches of WH Smith, Tesco, Martins, Borders, Eason, Sainsbury's and all good paperback bookshops.

MILLS & BOON®

DON'T MISS...

BETTY NEELS
MATILDA'S WEDDING & AN INNOCENT BRIDE

THE ULTIMATE COLLECTION

VOLUME EIGHT

On sale 7th February 2003

Available at most branches of WH Smith, Tesco, Martins, Borders, Eason, Sainsbury's and all good paperback bookshops.

MILLS & BOON

Helen Brooks

Lynne Graham

Kim Lawrence

BUSINESS
Affairs

Three brand-new stories about falling for the boss

Available from 17th January 2003

*Available at most branches of WH Smith,
Tesco, Martins, Borders, Eason, Sainsbury's
and all good paperback bookshops.*

0203/24/MB62

Don't miss *Book Six* of this BRAND-NEW 12 book collection 'Bachelor Auction'.

Who says money can't buy love?

On sale 7th February

Available at most branches of WH Smith, Tesco, Martins, Borders, Eason, Sainsbury's, and all good paperback bookshops.

2 FREE

books and a surprise gift!

We would like to take this opportunity to thank you for reading this Mills & Boon® book by offering you the chance to take TWO more specially selected titles from the Medical Romance™ series absolutely FREE! We're also making this offer to introduce you to the benefits of the Reader Service™—

- ★ FREE home delivery
- ★ FREE gifts and competitions
- ★ FREE monthly Newsletter
- ★ Exclusive Reader Service discount
- ★ Books available before they're in the shops

Accepting these FREE books and gift places you under no obligation to buy, you may cancel at any time, even after receiving your free shipment. Simply complete your details below and return the entire page to the address below. *You don't even need a stamp!*

YES! Please send me 2 free Medical Romance books and a surprise gift. I understand that unless you hear from me, I will receive 4 superb new titles every month for just £2.55 each, postage and packing free. I am under no obligation to purchase any books and may cancel my subscription at any time. The free books and gift will be mine to keep in any case.

M3ZEA

Ms/Mrs/Miss/Mr ....Initials...................................
BLOCK CAPITALS PLEASE

Surname ....

Address ....

....

....Postcode...............................

Send this whole page to:
UK: FREEPOST CN81, Croydon, CR9 3WZ
EIRE: PO Box 4546, Kilcock, County Kildare (stamp required)

Offer valid in UK and Eire only and not available to current Reader Service subscribers to this series. We reserve the right to refuse an application and applicants must be aged 18 years or over. Only one application per household. Terms and prices subject to change without notice. Offer expires 30th April 2003. As a result of this application, you may receive offers from Harlequin Mills & Boon and other carefully selected companies. If you would prefer not to share in this opportunity please write to The Data Manager at the address above.

Mills & Boon® is a registered trademark owned by Harlequin Mills & Boon Limited.
Medical Romance™ is being used as a trademark.